ROGUE VENDETTA

ROGUE VENDETTA

A WESTERN DOUBLE

UZZIAH MOUNTAIN MAN
BOOK ONE

J.J. BONHAM

WOLFPACK
PUBLISHING
— EST 2013 —

Rogue Vendetta: A Western Double
Paperback Edition
Copyright © 2025 (As Revised) by J.J. Bonham

Wolfpack Publishing
1707 E. Diana Street
Tampa, FL 33610

www.wolfpackpublishing.com

Paperback ISBN 979-8-89567-224-2
Ebook ISBN 979-8-89567-223-5

ROGUE VENDETTA

ROGUE VENDETTA

1

Saint Louis, Missouri, in the 1840s, was a rough-hewn place beside the Might Mo. A place of commerce and the mixing of the races. Blacks, Injuns, French, English, Dutch, Chinese and many more rubbed elbows every day. It wasn't about who you were, what color you were, or where you came from. It was all about money, whores, and whiskey. The middle of the three made money but were drunk and wasted as often as not.

Uzziah Ferguson O'Bannon's parents had come across the big pond long before the Great Potato Famine, and they wrote to their relatives and encouraged them to come to America, the land of opportunity, where men were judged by what they did and not to whom they were born.

Uzziah had left his family's farm in the Shenandoah Valley the year before. He had just turned twenty. He had helped with the farming and enjoyed the German families that surrounded them, but his heart kept yearning to go west. After hearing story after story of what lay outside the valley and to the west, he finally said a heart-wrenching goodbye to his ma, pa, brothers, and sisters and set out. There were eleven children in the family, and Uzziah was the oldest. It was time for him to make his own way.

He had put his sights on the far west, or at least the Rockies, but when he got to St. Louis, he got stuck in the—well, you certainly couldn't call it the glamour—but the excitement of what went on every day in that city. The law might as well not have been there. Murders, stabbings, shootings, and all sorts of beatings happened on a daily basis.

Uzziah was a big man, well over six feet tall and barrel-chested. He had wandered into a wharf-side saloon, and when it looked like a fight was going to destroy the place, he stepped in and either beat on everyone who was in the fight or threw them out of the establishment.

The owner, Charles Watts, was grateful. He had some whores who made him most of his money, and if O'Bannon hadn't stepped in, he might have been closed for a week, and he couldn't afford the damages to his funds. He liked his liquor and loved his whores.

When the fight was over and O'Bannon stood covered in blood and sweat, he was approached by Watts.

"Name's Charles Watts. I own this place," he said, extending his hand in friendship.

"Uzziah Ferguson O'Bannon," Uzziah said, Watts's hand disappearing into the huge mitt of O'Bannon's.

"Ya don't have an Irish accent."

"Born in this country."

"Sit down, I'd like to make you a business proposition," Watts said as he picked a couple of chairs up off the floor and settled them beside one of the only tables that hadn't been turned over.

Watts made a signal to one of the whores who had been hiding until then. She came over and set a bottle of whiskey and two glasses on the table. She had seen him do business like this before.

"This is Sarah, she's pretty, isn't she?"

O'Bannon had never been with a woman, and just the scent of her near the table had caused his member to rise a bit.

"Pretty, yes," Uzziah said as he took a quick sip.

This was going to make his coming deal with O'Bannon easier than he had first imagined.

Watts poured them both shots, raised his, and O'Bannon and he clinked glasses, then threw back the shots. Well, Watts did, O'Bannon sipped his.

"Where you work in town, on the docks?"

"Just got in this afternoon," Uzziah said as he took another sip and Watts poured himself another shot.

"How'd ya like to be my bouncer?"

"What's a bouncer?"

"What ya just did, son, my God, I never saw anybody throw people around like you did! Where ya from?"

"Virginia."

"Yer daddy a farmer?"

"Huge farm," O'Bannon said and took another sip.

"You ain't a whiskey drinker, are ya?"

"I like beer."

"Bring Mr. O'Bannon a beer, Sarah."

When Sarah brought the beer over, and it was nice

and frothy, Watts signaled with his head and Sarah sat on Uzziah's lap.

Uzziah at first looked like a giant spider had sat on him, and his arms involuntarily moved away from the whore.

Sarah put her arms around his neck and looked like an ornament on the big man's body.

"O'Bannon, I got me a proposition fer ya. Come to work here. We'll feed ya. Clarise is a great cook. You have all the beer ya like, and there are other benefits."

"Like what?"

Watts's eyes grew big as he pointed at Sarah.

"Oh," O'Bannon said as he dared to look down at the shapely girl sitting on his lap.

"I know ya like me," Sarah said, referring to the bulge in his pants, which had been throbbing on her bottom.

"Ya don't have to make up yer mind now, Uzziah. Let Sarah show you the rest of the place, and then we'll talk."

Sarah got up and, taking the huge hand of the Irishman, led him back toward the kitchen, then further back where the girls kept their rooms. Watts was one of the only whore-masters who actually had rooms built for the girls where they stayed and lived.

An hour later, Uzziah wandered from the back. He had a look on his face that told Watts he'd probably take the job.

Uzziah walked up to the table and looked at Watts.

"I'm hungry," was all he said.

"Clarise, stew for the gentleman," Watts said, snapping his fingers.

A bowl of stew was brought out. O'Bannon hadn't

eaten all day, and after three bowls he finally lifted his face up and looked at Watts.

"I think I love Sarah," O'Bannon said, and Watts burst into laughter.

"Uzziah, yer gonna love all my girls."

And that was that. Uzziah Ferguson O'Bannon started work that very day.

———

And so it was that a twenty-year-old Virginia boy became the bouncer in one of the roughest dives on the wharf in St. Louis. He had guns drawn on him, knives thrust at his belly, fists thrown at his face, but he had an uncanny ability to see what was coming next from any opponent.

And this kept on for nearly a year. It was his twenty-first birthday, 29 July 1841, when a man came into The Growling Catfish. He was a man like no other man Uzziah had ever seen. He was big like Uzziah and confident as the day was long. He was entirely dressed in deer skins and had a coonskin cap on his head. He carried an old Hawken rifle, which never left his side. There was just something about the man that Uzziah liked. It was early in the day, not even one o'clock, and The Growling Catfish was nearly empty. The whores were still all asleep, and Uzziah was there because that's where he lived.

He and Sarah had slept together for nearly a year. He had been offered the prizes of other whores, but it was Sarah he cared for. It bothered Charlie Watts because he didn't like the idea of any man falling in love with one of his whores. It nearly always brought trouble. But Uzziah had an ability to separate the Sarah he loved from the young snip of a girl that slept with all the wharf trash. She was his in his mind, and that was the only thing that mattered. He would have been hanging out with Sarah, but she had recently been sick, the flu or something.

"Can a man get a beer around here?" the man dressed in deer skins asked.

The bartender was in the outhouse, so Uzziah stepped behind the bar and poured the man a draft.

"Mighty grateful," the man said as he tipped the mug backward and drained it in one gulp. He wasn't showing off, just thirsty.

"Another, please," he said, and Uzziah poured himself one and the two men stood on either side of the bar sipping their beers.

"I'm guessin' yer the barkeep here?" the man asked.

"No, the bouncer," Uzziah said, taking another sip.

The man looked Uzziah up and down, even going so far as to lean over the bar and look at his boots.

"I could use a man like you," the man said after Uzziah poured him another beer.

The barkeep returned from his morning ministrations, and the two men took their beers to a table in the back.

"What kinda work ya do?" Uzziah asked once they sat down.

"Work! I don't work. I live in the mountains yonder." He pointed west.

"That's where I was headed when I came in here last year."

"That so?"

"Yes."

"So what's keepin' ya on this filthy wharf?"

About that time, a sleepy Sarah walked from the whores' quarters and up to Uzziah.

"Hey, O," she said and gave him a peck on the cheek. "Ya want Clarise to fix ya some breakfast?"

"Have her make enough for..." It was then Uzziah remembered he didn't know the man's name.

"Immanuel's my name, full name of Immanuel James Jones."

"Sure, Immanuel," Sarah said. "Always got enough for a friend of O's," she said as she walked away.

Uzziah turned back to Immanuel, who was smiling.

"It ain't like that," Uzziah said.

"Yeah, it is, nothing to shame a man. I once wandered into a Kiowa village and stayed there three years afore my Injun wife died whelping our third pup."

"We'll never have kids."

"Never's a long time, O," he said and took another chug from his beer,

"So ifn ya don't work, how do ya live?"

"Pelts."

"You're a trapper, then."

"Not so easily pigeonholed," Immanuel said, then added, "Also an Injun lover, Injun killer, lawman of the mountains, I don't like it when people mess with mother nature, and I have been known to be sought out to get lead outta men, and women, heal the sick, pray for the dead, and once, at Rendezvous, I actually preached a sermon of sorts." He grinned as he finished the beer.

"Two more," Uzziah said across the room to the barkeep.

———

They sat at that table after they ate a breakfast of channel cat, fried eggs, grits, and biscuits. Uzziah felt like he could tell this man anything, and he did. By the time it was required that Uzziah kick someone out, Immanuel stepped in when the man's partner tried to dry gulch Uzziah from behind. Immanuel clubbed the man with the Hawken and he went down hard. They threw both men in the alley, which was Uzziah's custom, and laughed about how both men had been amateurs to saloon fights.

When the evening was winding down, about two hours before sunup, Uzziah asked Immanuel a strange question, "Ya wanna sleep with Sarah?"

"You drunk, O?"

"Not more than usual," Uzziah said, then added, "She sure is fun to poke."

"You must be part Injun," Immanuel said.

"How's that?"

"The onliest man to ever offer me his wife, and let's face it 'cause she's as close as you ever come, if she was an Injun."

"Is that bad?" Uzziah asked.

"No, no, it ain't bad. It's just you either like me a lot or yer gonna kill me later."

Both men had a laugh.

Sarah walked up and showed another man to the bar. She saw those two still sitting there and walked over.

"You two are hangin' out like kin," she said, smiling.

"Give Immanuel a poke," Uzziah said.

"Sure, even give ya a discount. I ain't ever seen

anyone here that O liked," she said as she took Immanuel's hand off the table and helped him up.

"You sure, hoss?" Immanuel asked as she led him toward the back.

"Have fun," Uzziah said.

––––––

After the poke, Immanuel came from the back of the house sheepishly. He remembered the Injun who had lent him his wife and how, the next morning, as he left, the Injun jumped him. They fought like dogs until Immanuel killed the man. He wasn't quite sure what to think now of Uzziah's reaction.

Uzziah was ushering another man from the bar, one hand on his collar and the other grabbing his belt, when Sarah and Immanuel walked out. Immanuel sat back down at the table where they'd been sitting all day long. When Uzziah came back in from throwing the man out, he sat back down, and Sarah brought both the men a beer.

"Sarah's good, ain't she?" was all Uzziah said as he took a healthy swig from the beer mug.

"Damn, partner, yer something else," Immanuel said, slapping him on the back.

––––––

The three of them spent the rest of the summer like that. But when the autumn winds were blowing through St. Louis, Immanuel turned to Uzziah one afternoon when he, Uzziah, and the whore had gone on a picnic. It was a Sunday. Lying up on the hills surrounding the port city, they could hear the church bells peeling out noon.

"You ever go to church, Mr. Jones?" Sarah sheepishly asked the big mountain man.

"Not for a long time, little sister," he said, then added, "but I ain't disparaging those who do. You got to find God where ya find him."

"And you find him where, big man?" Uzziah asked.

"You know where. In the mountains mostly, when the shakies are turning the golden of the streets of heaven and the tops of the mountains are retaining the first snow, well, there ain't nothin' like it, old son."

Uzziah looked at Sarah, who looked at the two men.

"Let's go with Mr. Jones to the mountains," she said, poking Uzziah in the leg with a chicken bone.

"What?!"

"She's smarter than she looks, ain't she, old son?"

"You wouldn't mind?" Uzziah asked politely.

"Mind, hell. She's a good cook, I'm probably better, but having a little quim up there when the nights get cold, and you and me sharin' the way we been doing. I could teach you how to set traps, and gather the pelts, how to hunt fer yer food, our food. Old son, we would be in paradise."

"Ain't there Injuns?"

"There's Injuns here," Immanuel said.

"Yeah, but mostly drunk ones."

"Sure enough that, but yeah, we'll run into trouble just like you can run into trouble here. Ya just deal with it and that's that. I knows the medicine ways, and have collected so many herbs and treatments up at my cabin."

"You got a cabin?" Sarah asked wide-eyed.

"Yeah, little sister, and it ain't too shabby, neither."

"Come on, O, let's go. We'll just tell Charlie we're goin' and do it!" she said, almost shouting with glee.

"Don't he own you in a way?" O'Bannon asked, sort of looking at her sideways.

"Well, he took me off the street when I was a kid, showed me the ropes, yeah, in a way, I owe him, but I'm sure I can buy him out."

"What say you, future-mountain-man?" Immanuel asked, and then he gave a terrible cry, "Wagh!"

Both Sarah and Uzziah looked at him like he was crazy.

"That's what we mountain niggers do when we're excited. You try it, O, come on!"

"I'd feel silly," O'Bannon said and almost blushed.

"Wagh!" Sarah screamed, but it sounded like a baby in trouble.

"Hey, come on, even our gal is willin' to try!"

"Wagh!" Uzziah yelled.

"Too much in the throat, partner, got to come from yer nether regions like this. WAGH!"

The *wagh* echoed from the other side of the valley.

Uzziah stood and took several deep breaths like he was going to swim underwater, then he let it go!

"WAGH!!!"

Uzziah looked surprised and pleased.

"Ya got it, old son, now, all we's got to do is leave!"

2

When they got back to The Growling Catfish, everyone was surprised when Sarah just went right up to Charlie Watts and told him her plan. The man might have wanted to keep her, she was a damn good whore, but when his eyes drifted over to the two big men, he probably thought it best to let her go.

Neither of them could hear what she was saying or what Charlie was saying, but when she screamed and hugged Charlie's neck, they figured the answer was *yes*.

The next few weeks, Immanuel took Uzziah around and got him outfitted. Proper rifle, proper clothes, proper everything.

He chose the Hawken, even though it was the same rifle as Immanuel, because they could use the small-sized balls and the same powder. Immanuel took him up in the hills and taught him how to shoot the big gun, and not surprisingly, Uzziah was good with it from the beginning.

"Damn, old son, ya a natural with the big bertha! Yes, sir, a natural."

That pleased Uzziah a whole bunch as he wanted more than anything to please the older man.

It had been decided between them that they would leave in two weeks, Sarah doubled up on her giving pokes and was dead tired, but the extra money would come in handy for the supplies they needed for the mountains. Plus, Charlie Watts did have a buying price for her to leave! When two weeks were done, they were to jump a paddle wheeler up the Missouri and then ride on over to the spot in the Rockies where Immanuel had his cabin. The whole journey would probably take another three to four weeks, or maybe more, if they ran into trouble.

Their last night at The Growling Catfish, Immanuel and Uzziah were sitting at the same table where they'd gotten to know one another. An officer of the law, one of the deputies of the High Sheriff, had come in, and he'd always wanted Sarah, but she was afraid of him. This time, he offered her more money than she'd made in the past two weeks. While he was waiting on her answer, she sauntered on over to the table where the two big men sat.

"I never gave this one a poke 'cause he's known as a beater," she said, and the two men looked at Randall Hicken as he was bellied up to the bar, telling the barkeep a story that was making the man laugh.

"Is he drunk?" Immanuel asked her.

"I don't think so, maybe, who knows?" she said, still a bit apprehensive.

"You seem a bit scared," Immanuel said.

"Look, he's offering her as much money as we've

been able to save, what could happen? We're here, he knows we're here, right?" Uzziah asked.

"Yeah, I pointed the two of you out, and he just laughed."

"He laughed, I don't like it, don't let him have a poke. Where we're goin' money ain't shite," Immanuel urged her.

Uzziah was looking at all the folding money that she'd been offered. Obviously, he handed it to her so that the temptation would be too great.

"Nah, it's okay. He wouldn't dare hurt her. Hell, he knows we're here, and we done seen the monies and everything," Uzziah said and gave her a little nudge in the back, sending her Hicken's way.

She looked at Uzziah with the funniest look, a look he'd never seen on her face, and for the life of him, he couldn't make out what it meant. Then, without another word, carrying the undersheriff's money in her dress pocket, she walked back over to the bar, where Hicken looked at the two men and smiled. It was a strange smile, and the two men would remember it for the rest of their natural days.

Later, when they heard the blood-curdling scream, both Immanuel and Uzziah were on their feet and going back toward the whores' rooms. There was no one to stop them because Uzziah was the bouncer.

The walls in her room were splattered with her life's blood. Hicken had used a hunting knife, probably a Bowie, to gut Sarah. He had left her alive.

"Honey, darling," Uzziah was at her side, holding her head in his lap. Her intestines were scattered all over the floor, and there was blood everywhere.

"O," was all she said, then her head dropped to one

side. Later, he wasn't sure whether she'd actually said her nickname for him or was just expressing her dire circumstances. That bothered him.

————

They did not go after the undersheriff, not right away. Everyone knew he'd done what he'd done, and it was even rumored that he had done that before, many years ago, in another river town. They put Sarah back together, and Immanuel sewed her guts back up inside her. They washed her body together and dressed her in a dress, which they bought the same day they buried her. She looked like an angel in white satin. They bought her a plot in the respectable cemetery up the hill away from the wharf, and it cost them all the money they had saved for their trip.

"It's only money, old son," Immanuel had said. "Besides, I got me a cache not far from where the cabin is. I's never leave anything in the cabin. We'll make it just fine."

They hired a bagpiper, and he played as the glass-walled hearse rode up the incline to the gravesite. There were two white horses pulling the hearse, and they had feathered hats on. It sure looked swell. The bagpiper wailed into the air the strains of songs like, Great is thy Faithfulness, The Old Rugged Cross, and finally at the gravesite, Amazing Grace. All the whores were there, as was Charlie Watts. The whores walked two by two like the animals into Noah's ark. Charlie Watts led them like he was the schoolmaster of a bunch of fun-loving children.

The procession was slow and meandered right

through the middle of the best parts of town. Respectable people hung from their second-story windowsills, shaking their heads and watching as the detritus—to them—of the city wandered through their neighborhoods. They had never seen anything like it, and they probably never would again.

Several Pastors from the bigger churches in St. Louis blocked the gate to the Old St. Marcus Cemetery. They had their Bibles in their hands and their arms interlinked.

"You shall go no further," the one with the long white hair said.

Immanuel stepped forward. He had his Hawken draped across the front of him. He'd bathed, perfumed his long graying hair, and wore Injun jewelry which he said was for special occasions.

"There's plenty of empty spaces up here in the cemetery," he said as he cocked the Hawken.

"Would you kill men of the Lord?" the white-haired one harangued.

"In a heartbeat, Padres," Uzziah said as he joined Immanuel, cocking his Hawken. "In a heartbeat."

The pastors stepped aside as the glass-walled hearse passed by, their lips snarling in indignation.

As the service progressed and Charlie Watts was reading scripture over the open hole with the casket ready to go down into it, Immanuel nudged Uzziah.

Uzziah looked at him. Immanuel motioned with his head up the cemetery into the trees. There stood Undersheriff Hicken. He was smiling.

"Later," was all Immanuel said as they ignored the bastard undersheriff and paid their propers to Sarah.

They all took a handful of dirt and dropped it on

the lid of the coffin. The first few handfuls resounded with a thud like something terrible was happening, and it was. The whores were inconsolable. Their crying and wailing echoed off the hills and valleys.

———

By the time they got back down to the wharf, it was early afternoon, and Charlie said he was opening up so that the whores would stop crying. Both Uzziah and Immanuel felt that anybody that got laid that day did so with a weeping whore.

The two men planned what they would do to the undersheriff. They both knew that once this was done, they could never show their faces in St. Louis again. But what did that matter compared to what that man had done to the woman they loved.

"Sa—" Uzziah was about to say her name when Immanuel's hand was cupped over his mouth.

"We're gonna do like the Injuns, once someone ya loved one has passed, ya never say their name again, okay, pard?"

Once the summer sun had set, and it was late in the day, Uzziah and Immanuel made their way to where the undersheriff lived. He was a family man, and they hid down from the house behind a hedgerow. They saw the man playing with his twin girls. They couldn't have been more than four years old and were both thankful that those pretty young things would not have to grow up with their monstrous father. God knows what he might have done to them.

When the house grew quiet and almost all the lamps were extinguished, they were about to sneak into it and grab up the undersheriff. He saved them the trouble by coming out on the front porch, smoking his pipe.

Uzziah turned to say something to Immanuel, and he was gone. When he looked up, he was dragging a knocked-out undersheriff off the porch and into the bushes.

They had the man tied to the pack mule right on top of their supplies. They weren't going back, and that was that. The mule brayed a bit under the extra load, but it wouldn't be for that long. They rode up to the first wood station for the paddlewheels, and not far from there, they tied the undersheriff to a tree, upside down.

"What the!" he said as he awoke and saw the legs of the two big men standing there.

"Well, now yer awake, we're gonna get started," Immanuel said as he approached the naked upside-down man.

"You two are in so much trouble!" he yelled at both men.

"Really," Immanuel said. "We was thinkin' you was the one in a tight spot," he said, as he castrated the man. He yelled like there was no stopping his yelling as the blood ran down his stomach and into his yelling mouth.

"How'd that feel ya no-good bastard!" Immanuel said, then he turned to Uzziah. "Have at him," he said, and the undersheriff gathered enough courage to beg.

"Please don't kill me!" he pleaded through his pain, spitting the blood from his missing scrotum with each word.

"Oh, we ain't gonna kill ya, Chief, yer gonna die from what theys call exsanguination."

For the next few hours, both men took turns peeling

the skin off the undersheriff's body. Uzziah started with his feet and pulled down toward the bleeding crotch area. The man screamed like he was in hell itself, and truth be told, he was. Sometimes, the tortures of hell begin before hell is even entered. By the time they got to his torso, he'd passed out, but as they were cutting off his nipples and peeling the skin off his chest, he reawakened and yelled and screamed till he was hoarse.

When they were done and all the skin had been peeled off what looked now like a mass of bleeding flesh, he was unconscious again.

"He weren't filled with much bravery, was he, old son?" Immanuel said as they went down to the river and washed off.

"The good news is, he'll never do what he did to—her again, or anybody else," Uzziah said, almost saying her name.

"Fer sure."

———

They camped by the wood station that night, waiting on the paddle wheeler. They could hear the varmints tearing at the undersheriff's body as he was fairly consumed by morning. Wolves, wolverines, woodchucks, and just about anything that was hungry had their fill of the bastard. Instead of it being a grizzly sound, they smoked their pipes in the darkness and enjoyed the fact that the woman they both loved was intact and buried in St. Louis, and this man's remains would never be buried in sanctified grounds, but scattered over the hills in various animal scat.

When the paddle wheeler showed up, they helped

the men who had come for more wood load the bins and were thanked for the help.

They slept on the deck of the vessel near the wheel and were lulled each night by the sound of the water being turned. Immanuel had said that the paddle wheelers were rarely attacked, and they made it as far as they needed to go with no incidents. The two men had gambled onboard the vessel, and Immanuel had won back just about all the money they'd spent on the funeral and then some.

"God saw what we done, and he blessed us for it," Immanuel said as they got their horses and mule off and rode toward the mountains.

3

They rode for two days with the mountains appearing no bigger than they had when they first got off the boat.

"How far is these mountains of yours?" Uzziah asked.

Immanuel turned to him and grinned.

"They's a piece. You got to understand that the great plains is called that because they is great, huge, tremendous!"

"Is it just the one range we can see, or what?"

"Old son, they's go on and on and on. We get lost in there, and there ain't nobodies can find us, that's fer sure."

They spent the night on the plains beside a small creek that meandered over the undulating small hills. Immanuel was acting strange and Uzziah wasn't sure whether it was because the old mountain man had somebody with him or what.

"Do I make you nervous?" he asked Immanuel.

Immanuel looked up at Uzziah, who had been putting together a fire for their dinner.

"No, no, no, it's just for the past few hours, I've had the feeling that we was being watched."

"Me, too," Uzziah said, looking around.

"Ain't no use looking. The ways these hills dip in and out of one another, whoever's watching us could be just a ways away, and we'd never see 'em."

"So. What do we do?" Uzziah asked.

"Build a big, big fire up," Immanuel said, and Uzziah thought maybe his new and only partner might be losing his mind.

———

They ate dinner, hard tack, bacon, and two cans of beans. Immanuel showed Uzziah how to clean up the pans and tin plates down at the stream, using the sand as a cleaning agent.

"Can ya smell 'em?" Immanuel whispered.

"No."

"The wind is coming from the south now, and they's back down that away. Close yer eyes and let out all yer breath. Now, sniff the wind that's comin' our way."

Uzziah did exactly as he was told, "My God, I do smell something, and it don't smell good."

"That's White man's smell. Sour like bad milk and grubby like maybes they ain't had a bath in some time."

"Now, I can't stop smelling it."

"I knew ya was gonna be a natural at all this. Come on," he said, and they walked back up to where the fire was now brighter than the sunset, which was spangled across the western horizon. They sat down close to the fire, the air was already getting cool. "Ifn they was Injuns, they probably wouldn't bother us at night. Most the tribes got some kinda religious thing about dying in the darkness. But they's Whites. They'll try to sneak in and do whatever it is they's gonna do," he said and he leaned over and whispered something in Uzziah's ear. Uzziah listened then nodded his head.

They waited for a long time before they started to sneak into the camp of the two White men. They were hungry, tired, and cold. All of it a dangerous combination. They had been traveling for days without food when they found the stream. Following the stream so they would always have water, they saw the pair of White men, and they wanted some food. Now, they were on their bellies, crawling like Injuns toward the fire, which had burned down considerably. There were two of them, and only one big Bowie knife. Their plan was simple. Sneak in, grab some grub, and sneak out again. By the time they crawled to the White men's camp, their bodies were cramped and cold. They just couldn't help it, it was second nature, they crawled over beside the campfire to get warm. The warmth of the fire caressed them like a blanket, and within minutes, both of them were asleep.

"I'll be damned," Uzziah whispered to his partner.

Immanuel eased over to where the two children were sleeping and placed blankets over them. They were probably brother and sister. Both under ten years of age, and both tow-headed.

The boy came awake with a start and sat up, the Bowie knife slashing the empty air around him.

"'Bout time ya smelled the coffee and bacon," Immanuel said.

The boy charged Immanuel, who backed off and laughed, placing his hand on the boy's head. He slashed the air and cursed.

"You son of a bitch, I'll cut you to ribbons."

Uzziah walked up from the creek. He'd gotten water to make coffee. The girl, who was younger by a year or so, was sitting where she fell asleep, silently weeping and watching her brother try to harm Immanuel.

"Son, ifn ya stop fer a second, I can finish this bacon, it's about to burn, and we can all have some breakfast. There's biscuits in the Dutch oven, what do ya say?"

The boy started salivating, the saliva running from his mouth like a stream.

"You leave sis, alone, ya hear!" He backed off from Immanuel, still holding the knife in a threatening manner.

"Hey, sis," Immanuel said, "ya hungry?"

They found out that the two kids had been with their ma and pa in a wagon train, but a wheel had broken on the wagon, and the wagon master was cruel and told them they would go on without them, just like that. The next day, when the children were down by the creek playing, Injuns had attacked their ma and pa. The children said they hid and watched as they did something to their ma that they had only seen their pa do, then killed and scalped both their parents and rode off in the direction of the wagon tracks.

"How many days ago was this?" Uzziah asked.

The kids didn't know, but the way they scarfed down the victuals, it was probably close to at least a week. As soon as the children were through eating, they fell back asleep by the built-up fire. It was still early morning and chilly.

"What are we gonna do?" Uzziah asked.

"Well, pard, we gonna find the wagon tracks. There's a trail nearby called, I believe, the Oregon Trail. We'll find that trail and follow the Injuns who are following the wagons." The kids had told them that there were only ten wagons, folks who didn't know each other, and when they'd left Omaha, once they were far enough away, the men, there were four of them, who said they knew the trail had turned out to be not so friendly.

"I hate to say this, pard, but this ain't the first time this has happened. Well, meaning people who can't, or won't wait for reputable wagon masters, leave with whomever, and then they all get killed and robbed."

"Ain't it bad enough, the rigors of the trail without yer own people doing ya in?" Uzziah asked.

"Yeah, of course, but people from back east, some of them are the stupidest people who ever walked the earth. We got to find this wagon train and see if we can save them from themselves."

———

When the children woke up, they managed to convince them to ride double with them. The boy, whose name was Billy, didn't want his sister, Karen, to ride with Immanuel, so he did. Uzziah put the slip of a girl in front of him, but Billy insisted on riding behind Immanuel, and when the old mountain man tried to take the Bowie knife away from the boy, he balked. They found the Oregon Trail where it bent down and headed for Fort Laramie. The fort was a haven for those traveling west, and a place to buy more supplies since most travelers had no idea how long it would take them to get to Oregon.

"They gotta do whatever they're gonna do before they reach the fort. Then, they'll probably pick up other unsuspecting wagons and ambush them after they lead them further west," Immanuel said, then added, "Besides, anybody stupid enough to leave for Oregon this late in the year has got to be asking for trouble. Either they get waylaid by Injuns, outlaws, or end up dying in the snows in the Rockies."

"Ya sayin' my pa's stupid?!" Billy asked as he stuck the Bowie knife against Immanuel's side.

Immanuel had forgotten the boy's pa had made the trip, and now he was speaking ill of the dead.

"Sorry, son, I didn't mean to disparage yer folks, honest," Immanuel said.

"There's the wagon," Billy said, forgetting all about what Immanuel had said.

Their folks had been dead a while, and their bloated bodies stank to high heaven. What the Injuns hadn't done to them, the weather, sun, and varmints had. Karen started crying and Uzziah covered her little face with his bandana so she couldn't see more than she had to. Billy jumped off the back of Immanuel's horse, Trevor, and when he got to the bodies, he began throwing up whatever food he'd managed to get in the past day.

The two men dug graves with implements they found in the wagon, and Uzziah made crude crosses by tying wang leather sticks to make crosses. They stood there over the graves of their parents.

"Ain't ya gonna say words over 'em?" Billy asked.

Uzziah went to his saddlebags and pulled out a Bible he carried. Immanuel looked at him kinda strange-like.

"You can read?" he asked his new and only partner.

Uzziah just looked at him and opened the book to Psalms.

"The Lord is my shepherd," he began and read the entire 23rd Psalm. Immanuel kept his head down, like Uzziah was praying, but every once in a while, he looked up with new respect toward Uzziah.

When it was all said and done, and they were back on the trail, Immanuel rode up to Uzziah.

"Can you teach me to read the marks on the paper?"

Uzziah looked at Immanuel. "Sure, I imagine there'll be plenty of time this winter for such a thing."

"I'm holdin' ya to it," Immanuel said, and Uzziah simply nodded his head.

———

Immanuel decided they would follow the tracks of the nine remaining wagons. After all, they had an obligation to help the folks who were in those wagons. No wagon master would lead a group of people toward Oregon if it was this late in the year. There simply wouldn't be enough time for them to cross the mountains before the snows would keep them there.

Immanuel figured the only thing these four were going to do was take the settlers far enough into the plains, then rob them, take their horses, and leave them stranded. Why else would they leave the folks with the broken wagon wheel? They were on a schedule to get to where they would rob the lot of them, or maybe there were others which they would join up with, and they would divide the spoils? Immanuel wasn't sure how it would go down, but he was certain that it wasn't on the up and up.

They went into a set of rises and valleys. All of a sudden, there was a bunch of gunfire, and both men spurred their horses to make it to the next rise.

There, about four hundred yards away, the nine wagons had drawn themselves into a circle, and the Injuns who had attacked and killed Billy and his sister's parents were giving the rest of the wagon train a run for their money. There must have been about forty Injuns, and taking his spyglass from his saddlebag and scoping them out, Immanuel grunted.

"What is it?" Uzziah asked.

The two children were lying along the top of the ridge, as were the men, and all they could think about were the friends they'd made in the wagon train.

"More like who is it?"

"Well, who is it, then?" Uzziah asked.

"We gotta help 'em. We got friends down there," Billy said.

"They're Blackfeet. Don't know what they're doing this far south, probably a renegade band, and yes, Billy, we're gonna help 'em."

"Well, let's go then!" Billy insisted.

"Come on!" Karen joined in the argument.

"Billy," Immanuel cut in, "can you count?"

"Sure!" he said, seeming offended that anyone would ask.

"Then, put this glass to yer eye and tell me how many Injuns ya see down there?"

Immanuel helped Billy till he could see properly, then he started counting. When he got to twenty, he stopped and looked at Immanuel.

"They's circling the wagons, and I mighta counted some more than once, but there's a passel more than you two."

"Get yer Hawken, Uzziah," he said, then he turned to Billy and Karen. "That's why we're gonna help from up here."

"They're too far away, nobody can shoot that far!" Billy protested.

"You watch," Immanuel said as he set the sights on both Hawken rifles, then handed Uzziah's back to him.

"Now, when we start shootin' them Injuns gonna be lookin' for where they gettin' hit from. You kids stay down once we start."

Both men took their Hawkens, and lying down, they sighted by using the crest of the hill as a balance for the rifles.

Uzziah had never fired at men at this range, but he reasoned it was best to shoot at an Injun who was coming around the circle of the wagons from the left. They were all circling in a counterclockwise manner. So Uzziah waited till the next Injun was making that part of the clock at about nine o'clock. He would be traveling that part of the clock before he turned at six o'clock. He fired, and the Hawken came back into this shoulder. It was a good feeling.

———

Back down at the wagons, that particular Injun flew backward off his horse. The report of the Hawken was heard, but at that distance, the wind played with the sound, and all the settlers were firing, and so were the Blackfeet.

Fairly soon, the settlers noticed that Injuns were dying at an accelerated rate.

One of the bad hombres, Matthew Cash, turned to his partner. "Look up there about two-tenths of a mile toward those hills. Tell me I'm not seeing things."

Matt's partner looked and was rewarded with a puff of smoke, and a second later, another Blackfoot flew off his horse.

"Matt, we got long rifles up on the hill, and they's damn good shots!"

Fairly soon, the Blackfeet realized they were losing more braves than they could afford. The leader yelled up something and all of them joined him as they rode off toward the west.

"Who'd we lose?" Matt asked.

The man who was one of his three pards pointed to Harry, who lay dead across a wagon wheel, an arrow through his throat. He'd bled to death. The other three wagon masters told the settlers to stand by their wagons and see if the Blackfeet came back. The settlers had no idea that they'd received a bunch of help from quite a bit less than a mile away.

The three men, Matt, his brother, Wells, and Peter

Franklin, stood by crossed wagon tongues and watched to see who was going to ride out of the hills to the east of them. In about ten minutes, they saw dust blowing from over there and the two horses who were making the dust.

The two men seemed to be riding double. Finally, one of the settlers saw what was happening.

"Is it more Injuns?" he asked, concerned, getting the others around him to come and watch with him.

"No," Matt said, "it ain't Injuns."

"Should we be prepared to fight them?" the settler asked.

"They's got the Patterson's children with 'em," an older man said, who was holding binoculars to his eyes. At that, everyone who had expected them to catch up before now came over and watched.

Uzziah, with Karen riding in front of him, and Immanuel, with Billy riding behind, came up and whoaed their horses. Before anyone could say anything, the two kids jumped off the horses and ran into the arms of other awaiting children.

"Where'd ya find them?" Matthew, the leader of the bad hombres, asked.

"They found us, actually," Immanuel said. He had warned Uzziah that he'd better have a pistol under his coat and be ready to shoot if things turned south. Immanuel had bought two Patterson .36 calibers back in St. Louis after he'd sold his pelts. He'd dug the second one out of his saddlebags and handed it to Uzziah.

"Lucky for them, huh?" Matthew said, then added, "Well, we'll take care of 'em now. Many thanks for bringing them to us."

"It don't work that way," Immanuel said, his hand already encircled around his pistol.

"What don't work that way?" Matthew asked, but looking to his other two partners, whose rifles moved up a notch and hands swiped away coattails from their revolvers.

"We ain't handing those two lovely children over to you murderin' bastards," Immanuel said.

"Hey, that ain't no way to talk about our wagon masters!" the settler who had first seen them said.

"If I was you, pilgrim, I'd stay out of this," Uzziah said, hoping he could hit one of the three from his position on his horse. The good thing was he'd be shooting down, and missing would only put slugs in the ground.

"Stay outta what?" Matt said too loud, and all three of them went for their weapons. Rifles were coming up, pistols coming from behind coats.

It seemed to Uzziah that there were about fifteen shots in a matter of five seconds. And when he looked, the three men who had drawn on them were staggering backward with blood draining onto their clothes.

"Look what they done!" the settler said and started to raise his rifle.

"You're dead ifn ya do that," Uzziah said as he raised the Hawken up, aimed at the man's heart.

Uzziah's horse made a terrible sound, then stumbled.

"Damnation!" Uzziah said, "One of them got ya, didn't it, Molly."

The horse went down gentle-like, as if she didn't want Uzziah to get hurt in her death. Uzziah cradled her head in his lap as her tongue lolled out, and she breathed heavy-like.

Immanuel walked over with his pistol.

"No, she don't like guns, I'll do it," he said as he took his Bowie knife out. "You been such a good horse. Brought me all the way from Virginia," he said as he bent down and kissed her above the eye. Then, as if he were cutting bread, Uzziah slid the sharp as a razor knife across the horse's throat. She didn't even feel it with her other wound. He sang a negro spiritual, "Swing Low, Sweet Chariot," to her until she bled out.

———

The settlers were stunned that in a matter of minutes, the men they had trusted to take them to Oregon were lying dead or dying on the ground.

"These men were going to kill and rob all of you, pilgrims," Immanuel shouted.

"How do we know you're not the ones that are goin' to rob us?" the settler who had rushed them asked.

"They saved us, when we was lost, Mr. Trimble, they's good people," Billy said.

Another settler walked up and whispered to Trimble, "The boy's got a point, Fred. They wouldn't have saved those two children ifn they was bad hombres."

"Ya got a point," Fred Trimble said as he lowered his weapon, and Uzziah and Immanuel did the same.

The ladies from the wagon train had taken the wounded man and laid him out nice-like under the shade of one of the wagons.

"I don't know if this one is gonna make it, Fred," she said as she was binding up his wounds.

"Die here, or get hung at Fort Laramie, don't make no never mind to me," Immanuel said, standing over the man, who opened his eyes and looked at him, "You boys do this as a living of sorts?" Immanuel asked.

"You can go to hell!" the man said and turned his face away.

"Guilty as hell, that's what he is," Fred Trimble said, then added, "You boys gonna take us on to Oregon?"

Uzziah looked at Immanuel, who looked back at Fred Trible.

"No sir, we ain't wagon masters, we're mountain men, and we're headed back to the mountains."

"But we don't know the way to Fort Laramie, honest," Fred said, sort of scared.

"We'll take ya that far, right, Immanuel?" Uzziah asked his new partner.

"Yeah, of course, it's on our way."

———————

The great fear among the settlers going to Oregon was that the Injuns, the Blackfeet, as Immanuel explained to them, were going to come back and attack again. Immanuel let them know that as long as he and Uzziah were with them, that wasn't likely. He also explained to Fred Trimble that no wagon master worth his salt would have tried to take any wagons west at this time of the year. When they got to Fort Laramie, they would have to winter there.

When Fort Laramie came into view, the settlers were cheering from their wagons like they'd made Oregon already. The men had beat themselves up a bit, letting those four men take them in like that, and most of the money they'd spent was found either on the dead bodies or on the man who looked like he might make it.

Once the situation was explained to the captain of the fort, he went and talked with the lone survivor of the bad hombres.

"Now, we don't cotton to men doing to women and children what only one man should do to another, so, if what these people are saying about you is true, well, I got no alternative than to hang you at dawn tomorrow. Ya'd best make peace with your Maker."

"I ain't had no trial, ya can't just hang a man," the last of the bad hombres said.

"What's yer name, son?" the captain asked.

"Peter Franklin, why?"

"Well, Peter Franklin, at dawn tomorrow, you will be hanged by the neck until dead."

And that was the last of it. Word got around the remaining nine wagons, and the next morning all the settlers and their kids were lined up along the western stockade fence. A rope had been attached to one of the main supporting logs of the stockade fence and a hangman's noose fashioned by someone, who knew how, or maybe they kept it around and used it when they had to.

Peter Franklin was walked up the ladder to the place where he'd be dropped. He barely made it up the ladder, his health was so suspect. Whatever the settler women had done to keep him from bleeding had opened up again, and blood was running down his legs when they put the noose around his neck.

"Do ya have any last words?" the captain asked him.

"This ain't right! I'm being lynched by the US Army and—"

The captain had had enough, he pushed him off the walkway that surrounded the fort, and his hands went up to grab the noose, but he only managed to get one hand between the rope and his neck. But it strangled him just the same. The fingers on that hand turned purple, then black, then his face turned the same and he spun in the wind.

"Cut him down," the captain ordered.

Uzziah offered to bury the man outside the fort, and the captain took him up on it. He and Immanuel tied the body to the man's horse, and they walked out a ways from the fort. As they were digging the hole, Billy came running out.

"What ya doin out here, son?" Uzziah asked.

"I wanna go to the mountains with you and the old man," he said quite frankly.

Immanuel's head snapped in Billy's direction. "Who ya callin' old, son?"

"You," Billy said simply.

"Well, Billy, we'd be glad to have ya come with us, but someone's got to take care of your sister, Karen, right?"

"Can't she come, too?"

"Ya ever heard of any mountain women?" Immanuel asked Billy.

Billy thought for a moment, then he looked down at the ground.

"Yeah, well, I ain't either," Immanuel said.

They had the body wrapped in some tarp the captain had given them. They lowered into the hole and were about to throw the dirt over him when Billy spoke up.

"Shouldn't we say something over the grave?"

"Son, this is the man who left you and yer parents for the Blackfeet to toy with," Immanuel told the boy.

"Yeah, but I liked him when we thought they were all right. He gave me some candy once. That ought to count for something, right?"

Immanuel and Uzziah looked at each other.

"Yeah, candy ought to count for something," Uzziah said.

"Can ya read from yer Bible, Mr. Uzziah?" Billy asked.

They stood there, and Immanuel was wondering what Uzziah was going to do since his Bible was back at the fort. He had taken one of the bad hombres's horse as his own, a paint that he decided to call Josey. Immanuel knew just where the Bible was in Uzziah's saddlebags.

Uzziah stood holding Billy's hand and it was like he was reading, but there was no book in front of him. Immanuel couldn't believe it. He read the whole Psalm without having the book to read it from. Billy was happy and he ran ahead of the two men going back to the fort.

"How'd ya do that?"

"What?" Uzziah asked.

"How'd ya read from the book when it was yonder in yer saddlebags?"

"I memorized that Psalm years ago, think I've known it since I was ten years old."

"Well, I'll be damned, not only can ya read, but ya done save some of the reading in yer head," Immanuel said, looking at Uzziah with newfound respect.

4

Uzziah and Immanuel got up early the next day. They wanted a head start for the mountains, it was already snowing up there, and Immanuel was a bit worried about getting to his cabin before the snow got too deep. They enjoyed the last of a rope-suspended mattress, and when they went to get the horses and the pack mule, the two kids were waiting for them at the fort stables. In fact, they had been waiting all night, because they'd gathered up whatever possessions the other settlers had given them, probably cast-offs from their kids. It looked like Billy had gathered everything together in a sheet and tied it at the top. Both of them were asleep on the hay.

Uzziah turned to Immanuel and put his index finger to his lips. They tiptoed around the kids and were taking the horses from the stables when Billy awakened.

"Yer gonna leave without us, ain't ya?"

Karen was up now and rubbing her eyes. "Please," she said, "we go with you."

Uzziah and Immanuel looked at each other, and then back to the kids.

"Look, kids, we got miles and miles before we get to my cabin, and then there's gonna be so much snow to go through, you wouldn't believe it."

"We love snow," Karen assured them.

"Truth is, we ain't never seen it," Billy said. "But I'm sure we'll like it," he said, smiling.

Uzziah put his hand out and put it on top of Karen's head. Billy came and hugged Immanuel around the waist. The two men looked at each other, both of them knowing they were about to break some hearts. But what could they do?

Uzziah bent down and Karen rushed into his arms. He held her and spoke, "We're gonna come back in the spring and lead your wagon train to Oregon," he said and was looking at Immanuel, who just shook his head.

"You promise," Billy said, looking up at Immanuel.

"Yeah, we promise. If yer still here when we get here, we'll take ya. But ya got to promise that if the other wagons leave with another wagon master, you'll go with them, okay?"

"But what if they're bad men like the others?" Karen asked, then added, "Ya don't want us to go then, do ya?"

"The captain will know if they're legit. If he says they're okay, you go with 'em," Uzziah assured them.

Both kids gathered together with their little arms around each other's waists, then they both broke into tears. They weren't screaming and crying, just silently crying, which, to Uzziah, was worse than making a scene.

"Come on, Pard, we got miles to go," Immanuel reminded him.

They saddled up and Immanuel did not look back at the kids, but Uzziah, liking children the way he did, having so many brothers and sisters, he did look back.

There they stood, tears still running down their little cheeks and their hands waving goodbye. Uzziah waved back and they were lost as the men at the gate closed it behind them, and neither of them ever saw Billy or Karen again.

———

As they rode along, Immanuel would point out various medicinal plants that he had gathered over the years. Some of them, just a few, Uzziah knew about, but the others were new to him. Sometimes, Immanuel would get down and show the difference between the plants when they were dried and when they were in their natural state.

"Aren't we in a hurry, like we told the kids?" Uzziah asked.

"Well, yeah, and no. If yer going to be a mountain man, ya have to learn certain things. Those things, as they're right in front of us, need to be pointed out to you, so when a learning moment appears, I'm gonna take advantage of it."

It made sense to Uzziah, and he dropped the idea that they were in a hurry. Maybe they were only in a hurry to get away from the kids. There was a sense in which both of the mountain men loved those kids, and they understood that the kids wanted to be with them because they felt safe.

The rest of the day, they must have stopped at least fifteen times. Finally, Uzziah took a little notebook that he had and started making notes. Immanuel looked at him and shook his head in agreement with the fact that the man was recording some of these things.

That night, they had gotten closer to the mountains, but they were still a couple days' ride away. They hadn't seen any buffalo, and that worried Immanuel. He knew there were extensive herds all over the plains, so it puzzled him not to even see some from far away.

As Uzziah was making the camp, Immanuel rode around a ways from where they'd camped under some cottonwood trees and close to a stream, probably a tributary of the North Platte. He found plenty of buffalo chips further west, but they were all desiccated by the sun, there were no fresh ones. Off in the distance, much further west, he saw the beginning of thunder clouds, they were building strongly toward the heavens. It looked like it was going to be one big storm.

When he got back to the camp, Uzziah had set up dinner and it was ready. Evidently, Uzziah had used his bow and arrow that he'd bought at Fort Laramie. There was a jackrabbit over the spit on the fire, and Immanuel hadn't heard a shot.

"Did you use the bow to take down the rabbit?" he asked.

"Yeah," Uzziah said.

"But you just bought it."

"Not the first one I've owned," Uzziah explained as he dropped coffee into the boiling water in the coffee pot.

"Back east?"

"Yeah, there was this old Rappahannock Injun who

worked for my pa from time to time. He taught me when I was a bit older than Billy."

"And you remembered enough to get a jackrabbit on the run?!"

"No, no, he was busy watching something else, standing as still as a picture."

"Oh," was all Immanuel said, but he realized maybe there was less to teach this young man than he'd first imagined.

They ate the rabbit right off the spit, which Uzziah had stuck in the ground between them. They had beans, bacon, and biscuits, which Uzziah had made in his Dutch oven. As they were both sopping up the gravy, which his protégé had made from the drippings he gathered as the rabbit cooked, they looked at each other and laughed.

"Young son, you are a good cook, and that alone goes a long ways in getting on my good side," he said to Uzziah.

"Thanks, pard, that means a lot to me," Uzziah said, wiping his mouth with his bandana.

"In fact, it was so good, I'm cleanin' up," Immanuel said as he grabbed the tin plates and went to the stream.

By the time they got to their bedrolls, it had mostly turned dark, and they watched the lightning strikes, which were getting closer. Immanuel had been counting between the flashing of the lightning and the sound of the thunder. The storm was only ten miles away and coming their way.

"Better put yer vulcanized gear over you, the rain'll be here soon if it don't veer off," he said as he shook out his vulcanized tarp and spread it over him.

"What's vulcanized mean?" Uzziah asked.

"It means yer gonna get wet," Immanuel said as he laughed and rolled over.

———

Uzziah did get wet. No matter which way he turned it seemed the rain got him wet. Lucky for one of them that they had vulcanized rain gear. Immanuel was sound asleep and the booming thunder didn't seem to bother him at all. Then, Uzziah felt the ground shaking like the last thunderclap had been so violent that the earth was trembling still. But that was impossible. He walked to the rise opposite the river and could hear something like a freight train in the distance.

The rain was whipping into his face, and he had to put his hand up to keep it from stinging. Suddenly, there was a flash of lightning, and what he saw was incomprehensible. It looked like a sea of wet brownness was undulating at an incredible speed toward their location. Uzziah wiped his face clean of the rain, and holding his hand up to keep the rain out, he waited for the next lightning strike. When it came, he gasped. There were literally thousands of buffalo stampeding right toward them!

He rubbed his eyes, then, in another flash of lightning, what he suspected was confirmed. They were to be overrun.

"Immanuel, Immanuel, get up! Get up!" Uzziah said, shaking him.

Immanuel sat up, and just hearing what he heard, he ran to the horses and untied them from their highline.

"Come on!" he said as he grabbed his guns and as

much gear as possible and started climbing a cotton-wood tree.

Uzziah followed suit and realized he'd left his Dutch oven by the almost extinguished fire. He started to climb back down, but Immanuel grabbed his shoulder.

"No, young son, there's no time left," Immanuel said as the buffalo made the rise that Uzziah had been on when he first saw them.

The horses and the pack mule had already taken off running, not away from the buffalo as much as running away from their path of destruction.

Their camp was swamped with a myriad of buffalo. Everything was swept away. They held onto the branches of the two cottonwood trees which they had climbed as the trees were buffeted and swayed by the bodies of the buffalo as they swept by. Uzziah tried yelling over to Immanuel, whom he could barely see swaying in the cottonwood trees across from him. It was useless, there was nothing that could be heard except the thundering hooves of the massive herd.

Uzziah wished he'd looked at his pocket watch when this whole thing began because it was still going on, and it didn't seem like the herd was diminishing at all. And yet, he couldn't see, and most of the time, he kept his eyes shut because of all the dust swirling in the air.

———

Finally, he may have gone to sleep sitting up there in that tree, but finally, he couldn't hear anything, and when he opened his eyes, Immanuel was already on the ground, trying to salvage whatever hadn't been trampled by the herd. He was cursing and throwing stuff around when he noticed Uzziah was awake.

"You gonna sit up there all day and sleep? Come on down and let's get to looking for the horses and the pack mule. If we get discovered like this by Injuns, especially the Blackfeet, we're gonna be in a world of hurt, old son."

Uzziah got down and found some things which were now fairly worthless. His blanket, which he'd brought from Virginia, his mother had made the quilt, and now, there was barely enough squares for him to recognize it. He did see the Dutch oven kicked some yards away from their camp. He went out to get it. Luckily, made of cast iron, it wasn't damaged. The handle for the top was missing, but gloves would work to take the top off when it was hot.

"Hoop, hoop, hoop, hoop!" Immanuel yelled with his hands cupped around his mouth.

Uzziah jumped, thinking they were about to be overrun by Blackfeet Injuns, but it was just Immanuel yelling. He looked at him as if he were crazy.

"Is this another mountain man yell?"

"No, I dun trained my haus to come to this, ifn he's close enough to hear it," Immanuel said, and he started in again. "Hoop, hoop, hoop!"

"Hoop, hoop, hoop!" Uzziah started in on the call and pointed himself in the opposite direction from Immanuel.

Fairly soon, they heard a whinny, and coming from the direction the herd of buffalo had headed, they could see Immanuel's horse trotting toward them.

"Man oh man, the next time I can find some oats,

he's getting some!" Immanuel said as he started back in on the calling, "Hoop, hoop, hoop!"

His horse had their direction now and it was just a matter of time before he came in to where they were.

Immanuel stopped the horse. He checked the saddlebags, and it seemed everything that he hoped was still there, was still there.

"You need anything else here?" he asked Uzziah.

"Nah, it's all trampled to shite."

"Okay, we can't ride double 'cause of our girth."

"Is that a nice way of saying we're fat?"

"I guess. We'll take turns on the old boy. Let's go in the direction that the herd fled and see what we can see."

———

One walked and the other rode as the sun climbed into the top of the sky. It wasn't hot, but it wasn't cold either. Sort of the way it got in the plains when winter was on the way. The sun's arc would be shorter this time of year, so maybe they had ten good hours of light to find both Uzziah's horse and the pack mule.

The first things they discovered were items that had fled the sawbuck saddle and ended up trampled by the stampede. Thankfully, the items they encountered were not foodstuffs. Tobacco, made nearly useless by the hooves of the buffalos, and some geegaws that Immanuel had bought for some reason. Uzziah suspected they might have been for an Injun squaw that his partner knew, but then again, what did he know?

Uzziah was riding when Immanuel spoke up.

"Don't that look like a horse yonder?"

Uzziah pulled the long glass from Immanuel's saddlebags and opening it, looked.

"It's the paint, all right, it's Josey!"

They rode double toward the paint that Uzziah had named Josey, but every time he got off Immanuel's horse and started to walk toward Josey, he'd wait till Uzziah was almost there, then take off. He never went far, just far enough away so Uzziah couldn't catch him.

"Come on, Josey, come on, boy, here we go, here we go!" Uzziah said in his friendliest horse voice.

Josey would wait, wait, wait, then as Uzziah would reach for the reins, he would take off again.

"I got an idea. Come walk with me as we ride off. Horses are always herd-bound to some extent, he won't want my horse to go away," Immanuel said.

Uzziah walked with Immanuel as he rode away. He started to look around to see if Josey was following.

"Don't look around!" Immanuel said. "Wait till we've gone some distance."

Uzziah was worried that they were walking away from his only means of transportation.

"Whoa!" Immanuel said and brought his horse to a stop. "Don't look around partner, just stay looking forward."

In a matter of less than a minute, Uzziah felt the breath of Josey on his neck. He turned and took hold of the reins. Josey didn't resist.

"Ya see, pard, he didn't want to be left, neither by my horse or you! Now we gotta find that pack mule. Let's stick along the water source."

They rode for another two hours and were about to think that the pack mule and their supplies were gone or had been found by interested parties. The latter was

Immanuel's greatest fear. A man finds a pack mule all supplied up, he's not likely to let it go just because someone says it's theirs.

Immanuel decided to ride till after dark since that way they could see cookfires started up by someone else, if someone else was out there, then maybe find the pack mule.

The moon finally rose, and it was waning but still a gibbous so there was some light from it.

"Look yonder!" Uzziah said as he pointed down the tributary. There was a small fire burning about a mile or two ahead. They rode down fairly close, then tied their horses to a tree and walked the rest of the way. The wind was coming into their faces, and fairly soon, they smelled something like toilet water.

"Ya smell that?" Immanuel whispered in Uzziah's ear.

Uzziah nodded his head in the moonlight.

Then, the strangest thing happened, the woman that they had already smelled began to sing.

"I love it, I live it, and who shall dare, to chide me for loving that old armchair. I've treasured it long as a holy prize, I've be-dewed it with tears, an' embalmed it with sighs, 'tis bound with a thousand bands to my heart. Not a tie will break, not a link will start. Would ye learn the spell, a mother sat there and a sacred thing is that old armchair."

Her voice was lilting and clear as the night air they were standing in, and if the two men had, had their way, they could have stood there in the dark and listened to more of her singing, but the spell was broken when they heard a revolver cock.

"Who's out there? Ya better speak up afore I let go

of some lead to greet ya!" she yelled and was pointing the old pistol right where they were standing.

"It ain't nobody who's gonna cause ya harm," Immanuel said, then added, "Mighty fine singin' we heard."

"There's more than one of ya, I oughta just open up and let fly! Now, walk into the light or greet the darkness of death," she said as she stood and pointed the pistol in their direction.

They walked into the light of the fire, and it turned out the woman wasn't old or ugly. Her voice matched the fine features of her face, and her tiny figure was swamped by clothes much too large for her. Her auburn hair was crushed by an old slouch hat and she had taken off her boots and was standing in her bare feet. They were as small as a child's.

"Who are you, and what are ya doing sneaking up on my campsite?"

"I'm Immanuel James Jones, and this here's Uzziah Ferguson O'Bannon."

"Well, well, an Englishman and an Irishman. Can't say I care fer neither," she said, still brandishing the weapon in their direction.

"Could you point that hog leg somewheres else?" Uzziah asked her.

"I could, but I won't till I find out what ya want, as if I didn't know."

"We ain't here for that," Immanuel said.

"Then why didn't you call it by name?"

"That's our pack mule," Uzziah said, then added, "And that cooking bacon is probably ours, too."

"Ya ever hear the 'pression, finders keepers, losers weepers?"

"There's a Bible in the far pack, got my name written in it by my ma," Uzziah offered.

"Uh-huh, and I suppose ya want me to hustle on around that mule and look fer it?"

"I can look," Uzziah offered.

"You ain't doin' nothin' cept sittin' down by this fire and gently takin' those pistols outta yer holsters and laying 'em down, ya got it?"

They sat, and with two fingers, they pulled their shooting irons out and laid them by the fire.

"We done told ya our names, what's your'n?"

"Kate Singleton, what's it to ya!"

"Nice to meet ya, Kate," Immanuel said, noticing that the horse she had ridden this far was probably a plow horse, and her gear was mostly makeshift.

She wandered around to the other side of the pack mule and, opening up the pack, brought out Uzziah's Bible.

"Ya see, right there on the inside, right behind the cover, there's my name," Uzziah said.

"Can't cipher no marks. My husband kept me as dumb as one of his cows."

"Well, ya can see there's three scribbles there, right?"

"Yeah," she said, holding the Bible open with one hand and pointing the loaded piece at them with the other.

"Well, those scribbles are my name, my three names, Uzziah...Ferguson...O'Bannon."

"Maybe they is, maybe they ain't," she said, laying the good book down and studying the men who had wandered into her camp.

They spent the night once again along a tributary of the North Platte, or so Immanuel thought. She'd made a fire under some cottonwoods, and the smoke dissipated nicely among the colorful leaves. She'd fed them some of their own bacon, returned their guns, and decided it was time to sleep. If they wanted to stay the night, they could.

"But let me remind ya, ya come near me and my blankets, the onliest thing you pilfer from me is some hot lead." She cocked the old pistol, rolled over in her blankets, and slept just like that.

Uzziah awoke a couple of times, and there was nothing but the glow of the embers, which hadn't yet gone completely out. The woman, what she say her name was, Kate Singleton, she was still there, and so was the workhorse she rode in on. He kept thinking about what he could do to help her. He had an aunt whose husband beat the tar out of her almost daily, until he had a heart attack and died, although there was rumor his aunt had poisoned him. Nobody called the law, or the doctor, or anyone. They had a quick service and it was over. His ma had gone overboard like she had a tendency to do, and all his aunt's kids were smiling like there was no tomorrow. Well, there sure as heck wasn't going to be a tomorrow with the beater in it. Uzziah remembered that day, smiled, rolled over, and went back to sleep.

It was the coldest moment before dawn and the darkest. The moon had gone down, and all three of the occupants of the small camp were sound asleep. The man who came creeping into the camp had a scatter gun in both hands, and both barrels were cocked and ready to throw out death to anyone who defied him.

He was dragging a huge branch with many dried leaves on it. He placed it atop the almost gone embers, then backed away into the shadows. Within a minute or so, the flames shot high in the air, and Immanuel, who was sleeping closest to the fire, awoke.

"What in the name of hell?!" he swore loudly as he pulled his smoldering blanket away from the edge of the fire.

"Who is it!? Uzziah asked.

"What are ya building up a huge fire for? Ya tryin' to get the surrounding territory to come down on us!?" Kate was yelling and the loaded gun was swinging back and forth between the two men.

"Oh, it's so nice to hear yer lovely voice again, my dear," the man who had sneaked into the camp said, then added, "Don't anybody get crazy, this scatter gun will cut ya in two, and that's no lie!"

"Jeffrey!" Kate yelled.

"Jeff, ya got the advantage on us," Immanuel said.

"I sure do, and just lucky neither of ya was sleeping with my wife or he'd be dead."

"I ain't that kinda woman, Jeffrey, and ya know it!" Kate protested.

"Don't know what kinda woman runs away from home and leaves her husband without so much as a good go to hell?!"

"He beats me!"

"Like so many husbands who must train a wife," he protested.

"In his letters, he said he was kind and gentle, but he ain't! He's a bastard, and that's that!"

Jeffrey hit Kate in the side of the head with the butt of the gun and she went down like a gunnysack full of rocks.

Immanuel had his gun out and was shooting before Jeffrey recovered the scattergun, and it was blown out of his hands.

"Nice shot, partner!" Uzziah said and was amazed that anyone could do such a thing.

Immanuel walked over and put a finger to Kate's neck while Jeffrey was hopping around with his shot-up hand.

"She's dead," was all he said.

Jeffrey stopped hollering about his hand and looked guiltily toward the two men.

"You heard her, she was asking for it!" he yelled.

"Yeah, well, she ain't the only one asking for something," Immanuel said.

"Take me into the local authorities in Fort Laramie. I knowed I deserve it," Jeffrey said, holding his bleeding shooting hand and the other one together, wanting them to tie him up.

"Good idea," Uzziah said, and walked over and tied Jeffrey's hands together. Jeffrey smiled and sighed a sigh of relief.

"I had something else in mind," Immanuel said, looking at Uzziah.

They packed up all Kate's things and took their pack mule back. Jeffrey didn't say anything about the pack mule because he'd never seen it before. They headed back for Fort Laramie and Immanuel was in a foul mood. Going backward wasn't on his agenda, and he wanted to get back to the cabin. They had Kate slumped over the plow horse she'd taken, and Jeffrey was in his saddle with his hands tied in front of him. All of a sudden, he kicked his horse up and took off in the direction of the fort.

Uzziah was a good roper. He'd practiced long and hard back in Virginia, and folks made fun of him because roping wasn't exactly an easterner's skill. Well, it was about to pay off.

He rode up hard behind Jeffrey, but the man had one nice stallion, all black and sleek, and Uzziah could see there was no outrunning the man and that horse.

He threw a nice loop, and it caught Jeffrey around the shoulders and slipped down to his waist. When Uzziah stopped the paint, Jeffrey came flying off and hit hard. When the dust had settled, he spoke.

"Can't blame a fella for tryin', can ya?" he said, smiling.

Something snapped in Uzziah. He had seen his aunt's husband smile that same smile when she was all bruises, and it rankled him then, and now, well, he turned his horse away from the fort and kicked the paint into high gear. When he passed Immanuel, who was about to catch up, the older mountain man had a smile on his face.

"Now, that's more like it!" Immanuel yelled as Uzziah, the paint, and a screaming Jeffrey flew by.

———

Uzziah ran that paint until it was flecked with foam and his chest was heaving. He would have kept at it, but he didn't want to kill Josey. He looked once at Jeffrey, but he no longer resembled himself. He took his big knife and cut the rope that was tied around the mass of whatever it was.

He waited close to an hour before Immanuel showed up. He had the stallion that Jeffrey was riding, the plow horse with Kate's body slumped across it, and the pack mule. They were tied nose to tail in a neat line. The body was on the last horse since horses don't much care for dead people.

Immanuel looked down at what remained of Kate's husband.

"And I was only thinkin' of stringin' him up."

"This was more hurtful," Uzziah said and Immanuel broke into laughter.

"Hurtful, hurtful," he yelped between his gigantic laughter. "Son, you have a natural knack for understatement. I love it!"

They buried the woman, Kate Singleton, in a good deep grave, and wrapped her up nice so no sand or dirt would get onto her. They left what was left of Jeffrey right where he was. The buzzards were already circling.

Uzziah got out his Bible and read Proverbs 31:10-31 in which the author of Proverbs extols the good wife and how excellent she is, and how much her husband's heart should trust in her. They had gained a plow horse, a stallion, and a couple more guns. Uzziah took the scattergun, it was a Greener and a fine weapon. Immanuel wanted the stallion, but it bucked him off, and when Uzziah got on him, he was like a lamb.

"I'm guessin' that means he's your'n," Immanuel said ."If that be the case, I will take the Greener."

"Here," Uzziah said, not getting off the black stallion and handing the Greener over.

They rode away then. The stallion ridden by Uzziah, Josey tied behind it from the D-ring on Uzziah's saddle. Immanuel had the packhorse behind him, and they decided to leave the plow horse. But that dang plow horse had other ideas. Whenever they'd stop for filling their canteens or to grab some jerky and hardtack, the plow horse would show up, not out of breath, just slower than the rest.

5

They rode with some resolution and made the foothills of the Rockies. Uzziah had never in his life seen mountains like those. They were jagged and smooth, long-ranged and choppy. They were their own kind of mountains and now he was beginning to understand any man who could live there in the middle of winter would be a man well worth himself. Uzziah looked behind them and the horse he decided to name Samson after his older brother, who was strong as an ox but rather bulky when it came to just getting around.

"He still back there?" Immanuel asked without turning and looking.

"She's a mare and got a ton of heart, yeah, she's still back there."

"Well, ifn she makes it to the cabin, we can always eat her, ifn the winter is bad," Immanuel said laughing, then added, "Why you name her Samson ifn she's mare?"

"Let's get some things straight, partner. One, we will not eat Samson, and I named her that 'cause she's strong and unwieldy like my brother, Samson."

"Yer brother be real proud to have a mare named after him," Immanuel said, trying to get a rise out of Uzziah.

"Yes, he would."

Immanuel didn't get the reaction he wanted, so he started in on another tactic.

"So, why do ya think that Black will let you ride him and not me?"

"I'm prettier and weigh less."

"Whoa! Whoa! Whoa!" Immanuel said, and quite naturally, his horse stopped. "Not you, ya damn fool!" he said and kicked his horse back up. "Besides, I always and forever have put on my winter weight just afore the snows, just like a bear."

"You plannin' on sleepin' through the winter or just rollin' around," Uzziah said, smirking.

"Wagh!" Immanuel yelled at him.

"Wagh! Back at ya!" Uzziah yelled.

"We should be at the cabin in a day and a half. Glad it ain't snowed bad yet."

"How bad can it get?" Uzziah asked, seeing there were several inches on the ground already.

"You do not want to know."

"Actually, I do."

"So high ya can't get the cabin door open. I made a hatch on the side of the cabin so's we can get out when it's bad."

"How many feet is that?"

"Well, I built the cabin on a slope, so it takes ten or twelve feet to block the door."

"Damn!"

"Yeah, damnation is right. Since we got Samson bringing up the rear, let's stop early and do some huntin', what do ya say?"

"Ya think she'd let us pack dead meat on her back?" Uzziah asked.

"She won't even know it's there."

_____

They stopped early, there was plenty of light left. They made camp and walked out toward a swale where they'd seen a stream cutting a path. When they got there, Immanuel looked around and Uzziah had sat down on a rock behind some bushes.

"What the hell are you doing?"

"Huntin'."

"Well, this ain't Virginie, so ya better get up and follow me."

"Nah, with this here stream and the way I'm hidden, I'll have a couple kills before ya get back."

"Who is the mountain man here, I ask you?"

"You are, but I know how to hunt!" Uzziah said and looked away.

"Have it yer way, pilgrim," Immanuel said and stomped off.

_____

By the time Immanuel had made it back from his hunt, Uzziah was sitting around the fire with elk steaks sizzling over the fire. He'd made biscuits in the Dutch oven, and he'd gathered some wild onions, which he'd found under the skiff of snow.

Immanuel smelled the meat, walked over to the fire, and looked at Uzziah.

"You got one?"

"Three," Uzziah said, pointing to the upside-down deer, two of them and the elk, which was also suspended from the trees.

"Damn, son, you can hunt, can't ya?"

"I figured they would be okay," he said, pointing to the hanging meat. "The bears have gone to cave, haven't they?"

"Well, if they haven't, we're gonna find out."

They ate and Immanuel looked like he wanted to say something, but he kept it in.

"What's goin' on, partner?" Uzziah finally asked him.

"Look, old son, I may have some things to teach you about findin' beaver and curing the pelts and such, but it has occurred to me this night that this may be a two-way street. For example, how did you know there'd be game coming to that particular spot on the creek?"

"When I went down there to fill the canteens, I saw a mess of pellets and a bunch of tracks, that's how."

"And you didn't tell me this because?"

"You seemed sure you wanted to take a walk, and I didn't much care for a walk."

"Well, next time, hit me over the head and tell me what ya know, okay?"

"You got it."

———

They made the cabin halfway through the next day. Samson did not mind carrying the load of meat, and as Immanuel had said, she barely knew it was there. By this time, she, Samson, was keeping up with the two mountain men. Uzziah guessed because she couldn't keep them in sight unless she did. They still didn't have to put a lead rope on her, and that was a bit unusual.

The cabin deserved words said about it. It wasn't the usual crude shelter that a man puts together in order to stay out of the weather. Immanuel must have been working on the place for years. There was the main cabin, which, as he said, was built on the edge of a slope, and it would take twelve feet of snow to keep that big door from being opened. It looked, from the way the wood had weathered, that it was the oldest.

Uzziah guessed that after the main cabin had been built, Immanuel got a hair up his butt and built three other cabins, each with their own fireplace. All three came off the main cabin—one to the back, one to the left, and one to the right as you faced the main cabin. All of them were furnished with crudely made but sufficient furniture. Tables, chairs, beds, and lofts for sleeping when the weather was especially cold.

"This is a damn hotel," Uzziah said after he was given the grand tour.

"Well, on the outside chance that someday I'd have me a partner, I didn't want either one of us to get so bad with the cabin fever that we'd shoot each other. This way, we have places to go where we won't see the other one, and ifn say, you found yerself a squaw or even a White woman who was willing to go into the mountains, you two could enjoy yer nuptial bliss without making me feel like I didn't have any."

"That is such bullshit. I can't believe you even bothered to go there," Uzziah said, tilting his head to the side and looking at Immanuel.

"Okay, a man can get bored up here, and I like to build. Satisfied?"

"Sounds like the truth."

"But that don't mean that those other things ain't true, ya know?"

———

The next morning, they got up early and Immanuel took Uzziah to where he knew the beavers were. There were a couple of spots, and the water which Immanuel stepped into and led Uzziah into was the coldest water that Uzziah had ever felt. Immanuel showed him how to place the traps which weighed between three and five pounds.

"It's a good idea to place the traps at the end of the beaver dam. Where they go from deep to shallow water. Place the medicine on the trap," he said and took from his possibles pouch a pottery-made jar which had a stopper of cork in it.

"What's the medicine like?" Uzziah asked.

"Smells great, smell it," Immanuel said, sticking the jar under Uzziah's nose.

"Jees!" Uzziah said as he fell back on the bank of the pond. "What the hell is that smell?"

"Well, we have now proved beyond a shadow of a doubt that you ain't no beaver. Ifn you was, you'd be licking the medicine from the jar."

Uzziah came closer and sniffed at it. "What is it?"

"It's from the gland on a beaver. Some call it

castoreum, but some don't. Anyways, they like the smell, and with the smell on the trap, they think it's safe or even a good idea to go there."

Immanuel kneeled down on the bank and opened the trap by putting one knee on it and pushing the other side down.

"You do not want this thing to come back on you, son. It will flat hurt you, understand?" he said, and once it was locked open, he sprinkled some medicine on it. He carried it over to where the end of the dam was and sank it down in the pond.

"Now, this cheer chain is taken over to the bank, where it is secured with this piece of sturdy stick. You drive the stick into the bank and make it go deep, 'cause ifn it's not, he'll swim off with yer trap, and you not only lost a beaver but an expensive piece of equipment."

Uzziah was standing in the cold water.

"You do this throughout the winter?"

"Good Lord, no, we only trap beaver in the fall and in the spring. Their pelts are heavier and bring a better price in the spring 'cause they been keeping warm. The ones in the fall are okay, but not as plush, and plush is what brings the good money."

The next trap, which was to be planted, he let Uzziah do. Immanuel looked on and nodded his head up and down.

"Good job. The onliest thing I woulda done different was where you drove in the stake. Some people like to hide the stake, and I'm one of 'em, but ya may get by with just drivin' it there where the beaver can see it. Sometimes, the medicine does its work even though they're suspicious."

"How come the medicine don't wash off?"

"Oh, son, ifn ya get this shite on you, it will not ever come off. That's why ya have to be so careful. It's oily, and nothing will wash it off."

"We set all the traps in a circle which can easily be remembered. The last thing a trapper wants to do is change where he puts his traps or the order he puts them in. A wrong step by the trapper can cause him to be caught in his own traps, and there have been stories of trappers who were found dead by one of their traps or drowned."

"Grizzly," Uzziah said, and Immanuel came out of the water like he'd seen the devil.

"Where?! Where!?" Immanuel was asking as he swept the area around them with his Hawken.

"I meant yer story, it was grizzly," Uzziah said apologetically.

"Old son, do not ever say that word unless there is actually a grizz nearby, ya understand?"

"Shouldn't they all be to bed by now?"

"Shoulds, coulds, and woulds can only get a man kilt, boy. Remember, rely on nothing but what you see and hear. Notions otherwise are to be discounted."

———

Back at the cabins, Immanuel looked at Uzziah in a particular way.

"Yes?" Uzziah asked.

"Which cabin do ya want?"

Uzziah looked at him strangely.

"There's three, ya done seen 'em, so which one is yers this winter?"

"I like the one with the potbellied stove in the corner," Uzziah said.

"The southernmost cabin it is, then, good choice, ya get the sun first and longest, well done."

"Do you want that one?" Uzziah asked, not wanting to be stingy.

"Look, old son, I asked which one you wanted, and you chose. It's a done deal," Immanuel said, then added, "Now, you fix supper, and I wouldn't mind a repeat of what we had last night."

———

Immanuel might have had two suppers that were equally good, but he couldn't remember when. The elk steaks and the biscuits, Uzziah even made a gravy out of the drippings he'd saved from the steaks. There were no wild onions, but Uzziah saw something that looked like dandelions, and they were. He had eaten those as a boy when he went hunting by himself, so he pulled the almost frozen plants from the ground. Every part of the dandelion is edible, and he cooked them like greens. Immanuel was surprised at how good they tasted.

"Old Son, you are officially the cook for this party, make no mistake," Immanuel said as he picked his teeth with a straw he'd pulled from the broom in the cabin.

"Do we check the traps tomorrow?"

"Every day, Uzziah, every day. Come hell or high water. But first, we're gonna go get my cache, which I buried. Been so long it will be like opening a Christmas present."

Uzziah built up the fire in the potbellied stove and soon found out just how hot a cabin can get.

He stepped from the cabin to breathe some fresh air.

"I shoulda warned about the stove, it'll flat burn you out of there," Immanuel said. He was working on some horse tack.

"Anything else I should know about this southernmost cabin?" Uzziah asked.

"Check it for bugs and spiders, some are harmless, and some aren't," Immanuel said. "I done swept mine out."

———

Because it was still nice enough to spend the night outside, Uzziah and Immanuel slept under the stars again. It was cold, but they had a good banked fire, and whenever either of them got up to pee, they would throw more wood on the fire. By the time morning rolled around, Uzziah had the fire back up and was making pancakes.

They'd bought some sorghum back in St. Louis, and it would go fine on the johnny cakes. They were made from cornmeal, and the ones they didn't eat that morning they could throw into their saddlebags and eat on the trail. Immanuel had said that he had buried his cache quite a ways from the cabin, not wanting anyone observing what he was doing when he did the digging.

They checked the traps first, and not one of them had been stepped into.

"Well, some days you get the beaver, and some days the beaver gets you," Immanuel said.

"You talkin' about animals with big flat tails or women?" Uzziah joked.

"Both."

They rode for a couple of hours. The pack mule was tied to Immanuel's saddle, and Samson, the big plow horse mare, simply followed them out of camp. Uzziah had no idea why Immanuel would bury his goods this far from the cabin, but he was sure he had a reason. Immanuel had left a shovel sort of hidden behind some boulders, and when he reached back there to get it, a rattlesnake struck at him. The older mountain man was quick and grabbed the rattler behind the neck and brought him out to Uzziah.

"You like snakes?"

"Don't hate 'em."

"Well, learn to hate this kind," he said as he threw him on the ground and cut off his head with the shovel. "I hate 'em. You get bit out here and you're by yerself, ya just might die!"

They threw dice to see who would dig first. Uzziah lost and half an hour into the dig, he thought Immanuel's dice might be loaded, but he was going to let it slip. He dug for two hours, and still no cache.

"I told ya it was deep, my turn," Immanuel said, and about fifteen minutes later, he hit something.

"Is that it?"

"The edge of it, we's digging too far east," he said and began digging in the direction of his buried goods. By the time they'd dug over and up, it was getting later than Immanuel liked.

"I guess we'll stay the night and finish up in the morning," he said.

They ate the johnny cakes they'd brought from breakfast, and Uzziah made coffee. Neither man thought they'd be all day doing this.

———

In the morning, the coffee was reheated, drunk, johnny cakes finished, and Immanuel had some jerky he shared with Uzziah.

"I know you didn't get enough to eat," Immanuel said to Uzziah.

"I'll make it," Uzziah said, sore from the day before's digging. He started back in, and fairly soon, within a couple of hours, they had the cache pulled from its grave and were marveling at everything Immanuel had thought to save.

"There's enough here for a man to live all winter, I'll bet," Uzziah said, admiring his new mentor's savviness.

"There sure is," came a voice from nowhere, and then they heard two pistols cock.

When they looked up, the man, well, really, he was a boy, couldn't have been more than sixteen years old.

"Where's yer mama?" Immanuel asked him, and the boy shot Immanuel in the arm. The big man didn't go down, nor did he scream, but he gave a look to the boy that could have killed.

"More talk like that and I'll have to kill ya, mister," the boy said. "Name's Albright, Bobby Albright, but folks back where I come from call me Bob Bright!" He said it like the birdcall of the same name, Bob-white!

"It's only the masked Bobwhite that sounds like that," Immanuel said, wrapping his bandana around his arms where the bullet had creased him.

"So, we got ourselves a nature lover among us, do we?"

Immanuel just looked at the boy like he wanted to kill him on the spot.

"Both you hombres, drop your gun belts, and don't go near those Hawkens. Can't believe you two are still carrying that ancient armament. Don't you know they done made a lot better rifles than those pieces of shit?"

"I could drop you at six hundred yards with that there rifle."

"Well, good thing I'm standin' so close, ain't it! Besides, when men talk shit, and I know it's shit, I like to call 'em on it. You couldn't hit the broadside of a barn at six hundred yards with that ancient cannon. Now, load the mule and the mare both, and make it snappy."

They worked for the better part of two hours securing the loads.

"Why, exactly, are we doing such a good job on these loads?" he whispered to Immanuel. The kid was off smoking a rolled cigarette.

"They's our loads. He might take 'em to the plains, but that's as far as he's gonna get."

"How do you know he's going back to the plains?"

"Look at his boots, they're the boots of a dandy. He just comes up here to rob old men. Well, he's robbed the wrong old man, I can tell you that!"

"What are you two fat, old men whispering about?" the boy demanded, pointing the guns at the both of them.

"We're talking about how we're gonna kill ya. Would you like to hear?"

"Shut up! Both of ya sit by that big tree."

"This Ponderosa?" Immanuel asked.

"Is that what it's called? Yeah, sit down there."

The boy, Bob Albright, Bob White! Tied them to the tree with all the rope they had. It was a lousy job.

"I'm taking the black horse, he's mine now," he said to the both of them.

"I wouldn't do that, son," Uzziah said.

"I ain't yer son, and I'll do whatever I please," he said as he swung up in the saddle of the black.

It was rodeo time, and they had to give it to the boy, he slapped leather a lot longer than they thought he would, but eventually, he went flying into the air, and Immanuel sincerely hoped he'd break his neck when he hit the earth. But like a lot of bad people, he had luck with him and barely scratched himself.

"Don't think I'll take that one," he said as he brushed himself off.

When he rode out, he was on Immanuel's horse and had both the pack mule and the mare, Samson, tied to either D-rings on the saddle.

They rode double on the stallion, and it took Uzziah several minutes to convince Immanuel that the black wouldn't buck them off once he got on.

The rope was easily cut through with a knife Immanuel had in his boot. Uzziah made a note that he should start carrying such a knife in such a place.

They had to give the boy credit, he made it to the plains and out of the foothills, but they made it as far as the last of the foothills, and Immanuel had Uzziah pull up.

"Why we stoppin' here?"

"I told that punk boy what I was going to do, and by

God, that's exactly what I'm fixin' to do," Immanuel said as he fired a warning shot into the air. It took a while for the sound to reach the plains, but when it did, the boy actually got off Immanuel's horse and shot them the finger from both hands.

Immanuel was looking through the spyglass.

"Good bad boy," he said. "Got off my horse and he's making a perfect target," he said as he laid down on a flat rock and sighted in.

Meantime, the boy was dancing around and kept shooting them double birds.

When the Hawken fired, the booming sound traveled a bit slower than the 50-caliber chunk of lead.

———

Bob Albright had pulled his penis out and was wagging it for the spyglass when the bullet severed the aorta where it met the heart.

"What the hell," he said and was trying to put his dick back in his pants when he fell to his knees. "He done it, at least six hundred yards, I'll be..."

Whatever he was going to be, he didn't say, perhaps damned, perhaps dead, perhaps a monkey's uncle. Whatever he was going to be was lost as he hit the dirt in a face-and-dick plant. His efforts at modesty had failed. Dust shot up around him, and then the sound of the big gun sent the horses scattering a little ways.

That's the way they found him, face down. The boy had an amazing head of blond hair, which looked like his mama hadn't cut since he was born.

Uzziah was in a bit of shock when Immanuel bent over the boy and took his Bowie knife, scratched it across his forehead, and pulled the entire head of hair in one fast jerk off his skull.

"Bob-White!" Immanuel yelled into the sky, mocking the boy by making the perfect call of the Masked Bobwhite. He took the scalp and tied it to the reins on his horse. The horse did not object, which made Uzziah think that perhaps this wasn't the first time Immanuel had taken a scalp.

6

It was way too late in the day to head back. The time that it would have taken them to return to the cabins, they had spent chasing the boy, Bob Albright. It didn't matter though. They had the cache that Immanuel had so skillfully hidden, and tomorrow, they would be back at the cabins.

As they sat around the campfire, it was still light enough to see well, but hunger had overtaken both of them. As they sat there relishing some of the treats that the older man had sequestered in the cache, raspberry jam in jars—Uzziah had never dreamed anyone could make better raspberry jam than his grandma, but here it was spread over a biscuit that was piping hot. Life was good.

But all Christian men are taught that when things seem too good, sometimes, that's about the time that the adversary strikes. The biblical adversary is, of course, the devil, but then they heard the cries of the warriors and could see a party of some twenty riding toward them from the plains, they might as well have been red devils.

Uzziah jumped up.

"What'll we do?"

"Well, I'm not leaving this stuff, if that's what you mean." Immanuel had his spyglass out and was glassing them. "They're Apache, but I ain't never seen Apache up this far north. They must have followed that buffalo herd that nearly trampled us to death. I'm gonna count on them wanting what I got. You ride away on the black, they could never catch you, go now!"

"But I can't just leave you," Uzziah protested.

"You ain't leaving anybody, you're making what any good Cavalry Officer would call a strategic retreat. Go into the mountains, follow us when they take me—"

"What makes you think they won't kill you!?"

"I've been around these red niggers long enough to know a few things. A prize like this cache, well, they're gonna wanna take me to their leader, their chief, whoever's running this party and show him how brave they were and how much they counted coup, now go, now! Here, take the spyglass," and he threw the cylindrical object at Uzziah, who caught it on the run to his horse.

Uzziah looked up, and he would be lucky to outrun the party of Apache, which was getting awfully close now. He could hear the heavy breathing of their horses.

He jumped on the black, who crow hopped a bit, better remember, he doesn't like to be jumped on. They lit out of there like they were a shuck on fire.

"Yip, Yip, Yip," a bunch of them screamed and broke off to go after Uzziah and the amazingly fast horse.

Uzziah looked around and several of them were notching arrows and getting ready to let fly. He spurred the black on, and he found another speed. He struck out like the world was on a wheel and they were only jumping into the air, and it was the world that was spinning beneath them. The next time he looked around, arrows were falling short, and several shots from old rifles were fired, but he couldn't even hear the passing of the lead.

He ran right up into the hills, and he was so far ahead of them that he rounded a big boulder and jumped down with his Hawken. It was, of course, loaded. He spread himself over the curvature of the rock and beaded in on the incoming crew of Injuns. He'd show them it wasn't a good idea to follow him.

Boom! Crashed the Hawken, and one of the parties of followers' head exploded and the body rode on until it sluffed off his horse. The remaining Apache turned and headed back to the big catch.

Uzziah took the glass and, opening it, scanned down on the plains, expecting to see a magnificent fight where Immanuel would be killing as many of the Apache as he could. Instead, he saw his friend with open arms welcoming the braves who rode around him, who brandished spears and arrows and pointed rifles and old weapons at him. Then, one of them saw the blond, long scalp that Immanuel had just tied to his reins. He lifted the scalp and everyone there screamed into the evening air. They were pleased that a White man had followed their methods.

What the hell was going on? Were these friends of Immanuel? Had he killed one of the party of his friends, what would happen to Immanuel now?

Looking further, he saw him unpacking one of the sawbucks, showing the very interested braves what he had there. There was much celebration and hollering as they found a jug of whiskey and were passing it around, but in the middle of the passing of the jug, one brave fired his rifle into the air.

It was like watching a play from a long distance. He wished he could hear what they were saying, but then again, he didn't speak Apache. The leader of this raiding party was the one who fired, obviously. He got the jug back, corked it, and tied it back on the pack mule. He got them organized and the celebrating continued as they rode south.

It was as Immanuel had said it would be. They were taking him, alive albeit, and the cache to their camp to display the winnings they had secured for the tribe.

While it was still light enough for him to be seen, he kept to the foothills and followed them along the place where, for thousands of years, tribes and animals had walked along the beginnings of the Rockies.

It wasn't long till it got dark and he decided he was traveling over too much terrain to keep up, so he scooched down on the edge of the plains again. They were easy to follow even though the moon had not risen. He could hear their laughter, the sound of the bells on their horses, and the horse hooves—unshodden, mind you—but still making a sound as they rode over the grasses of the plains.

Uzziah was tired. He'd just eaten and he felt like sleeping, but he wasn't going to stop till they did. Maybe, mayhaps, he could find a way to rescue Immanuel, who knew?

They traveled all night. The moon had risen, but it was the waning fingernail moon, barely giving enough light to see your own hands. They would never ever see him back there following. For a bunch of Injuns, they sure seemed ignorant of what was happening around them.

———

It was the morning of the next day before they reached their encampment. Teepees were spread in a fan-like spread away from the banks of the river which both he and Immanuel thought was the North Platte.

A certain teepee was approached, and when the Apache who came from it emerged, everyone there yelled together, the women of the tribe ululating. There must be a total of 100 Apache or more. The women were busy curing buffalo hides, and Immanuel had been right again. The Apache had followed the herd all the way north and the winter for them would be a good one.

Immanuel's cache was displayed to the chief, he must have been a chief the way they all treated him. Everything was laid out to show the big man, and from what Uzziah could see through the long glass, the man seemed quite pleased. Immanuel was escorted into the teepee of the chief, and Uzziah wished he was a fly on the inside of that teepee.

———

Immanuel knew that Uzziah was following them. Every once in a while, he heard the distinctive whinny of the big black stallion, probably smelling some of the mares that the Apache were riding. That particular horse sound would have been lost to the others, having never heard it before.

The invite into the chief's teepee wasn't unexpected. After all, he had brought a great boon to them, and it would be rude for them simply to kill him instead of giving him thanks. Yet, Immanuel knew that just because they feed you at lunch doesn't mean they're not going to make you run the gauntlet in the afternoon.

Fairly soon, from what he knew of the language, which wasn't very much, and the things they were saying made him believe that they were the Bedonkohe band of Chiricahua Apache.

They had been living on the plains and deserts of the southern territories for centuries, and they had probably made the *road* that led from Mexico to Canada and ran along the eastern slope of the Rockies.

Food was being brought in, so Immanuel had been right, they would party before doing anything else. Some of the squaws who brought the food in were older, and then there was one in particular, much younger, and smiling at him like she knew him. She seemed to know the chief quite well. Could have been his daughter.

The food was mostly buffalo tongue and fried bread, although he did recognize the raspberry jam which he and Uzziah had enjoyed for breakfast the day before. So, they were already getting into the cache which he'd stored for the winter. He had to forget that and worry about escaping with his life.

When it was warmer, they moved the party outside

where a huge bonfire had been built up, and Immanuel was given the honor of lighting it. He tossed the burning torch into the built-up twigs, sticks, and logs and it whooshed into life. He wondered if maybe later he would be roasted over this same fire.

A young man came and sat beside the chief. He had very intelligent eyes, and when he spoke to the chief, the man really listened. There was a White woman among the squaws who brought the food when they were sitting around the fire. Immanuel nodded to her, but she quickly looked away. Finally, when the party was well underway, and the chief wanted to know something about this man who had been able to have such fine things around him, the chief had the White woman come and sit with them at the fire.

The chief spoke to the White woman, who listened intently, then turned to Immanuel.

"I—how do you say—haven't spoke this—way in long time," she said and blushed.

Immanuel was thinking that she was a whole lot prettier than when he'd first seen her. He was beginning to wonder what her life was like with the Apache, but he knew she had fared better than those she'd been taken from, who were most likely dead, scalped, and buzzard food long ago. Her Apache was good, or so it seemed to him.

"Where you come from?" she asked him.

He told her about being in Saint Louis and selling his pelts, then gathering up his cache. She told the chief, who listened intently, but not as intently as the boy beside him, who couldn't have been any older than ten years.

"Who man with you?" she asked him.

He lied and told her he was no one, just a man he'd met and helped him dig up the cache. He told them he was glad he was gone because now he didn't have to split the cache with him. When this was told to the chief, the boy at his side stood and pointed to the south and kept pointing there and saying something, the same thing over and over.

"What's he saying?"

The White squaw saw that everyone around the boy was paying attention to him and not the two of them, so she spoke freely.

"He Chief's son, Geronimo. He have special sight. He says the man you talked about has not left but is where he point."

———

To the south, Uzziah was unhinged by the fact that as he was watching them around the big bonfire, a boy had stood and kept pointing directly at his position. How could he have known that he was there?

———

"Do they believe him?" Immanuel asked the White squaw as the other braves were looking to where Geronimo was pointing.

"No and yes, the chief no believe, he tell boy to sit down, be quiet."

Eventually, the boy sat back down, and things returned to normal, although he, Geronimo, did not stop staring toward the south. Immanuel knew that's probably where Uzziah was because it was the only place with some cover. He certainly hoped that Uzziah was making a plan to rescue him because he was fairly sure that if he wasn't rescued, he would be the evening's entertainment.

The Injuns had opened everything in the cache. It was so typical of them. They had all the items spread out, and they were being admired. One Apache picked up one of the Roman candles Immanuel had kept to help him celebrate Christmas. He thought how wonderful those arcing bands of light would be and how loud the explosions would be when they reached the height that they would explode. Each of them had a fuse on them, and the Injun wasn't stupid. He knew what a fuse was. He lit it and held it so it was pointed at the chief's party.

Immanuel rushed over, and several braves brandished their weapons to protect whatever, but all Immanuel did was take the Roman candle and squash the fuse between his fingers.

"Tell the chief that these are candles which have special powers. I will demonstrate them tonight once it is dark. It is bad medicine to light them in the day," Immanuel said to the White woman who relayed the message to the chief. He grunted and seemed to scold the brave who had lit the fuse. He slinked away with his head down.

It was then that Geronimo gathered all the Roman candles and laid them at the feet of the chief, his father, who seemed very pleased that the boy had done so.

What happened next was meant for O'Bannon's eyes and O'Bannon's eyes alone. Immanuel got up and walked over to the Roman candles and then looked up right into the long glass that Uzziah was using. He was speaking to the chief, and Uzziah could see that the woman was translating, but his gestures toward the Roman candles and his expressive use of his arms and hands demonstrating their ability to fill the sky with wonders, well, that was all for his new partner, Uzziah Ferguson O'Bannon, and he knew it.

———

Uzziah would wait till dark, when the fireworks would be used, but he must get as close as he could to the demonstration of fireworks to carry out the plan that he and—he hoped—Immanuel James Jones had in mind.

Being late in the fall, the sun set earlier than summer. O'Bannon had crept down the swale made by the tributary of the North Platte as close as he could to the village without being seen. The young boys of the village were the ones watching the horses who were gathered along the river, allowing them use of the stream when they became thirsty.

Uzziah watched the boys who were watching the festivities up on the plains away from the river. You could tell by their movements that they didn't want to be there, that all they really wanted to do was be where the fireworks were going to be shot off. Uzziah wished he could get closer because when the action started up there in the sky, he was going to have to move in as quickly as he could without being noticed and grab Immanuel. They would exit the same way Uzziah came in, and going by the horses, they would grab Immanuel's mount and the pack mule and get out of there.

Above him, in the darkness of the night sky, Uzziah saw a tracing of something, and when he looked up, the rocket exploded into a chrysanthemum of sparkling lights. When he looked back down, his night vision was gone. Good, that would be exactly what would be happening with the Apache when they were watching the lights.

He ran down the embankment of the Platte, then as he walked up the bank, he noticed all the boys who were supposed to be watching the horses had run into the village, he could actually see the last of them high-tailing it toward the center of the teepees.

It was counterintuitive, but he casually walked toward the village, but everywhere he looked all eyes were on the sky and what was happening there. Explosion after explosion rattled the night sky, and the oohs and ahhs of the Apache echoed after every demonstration. If only the Roman candles would not run out.

Now, O'Bannon was walking up behind the chief's tent, and thankfully, Immanuel had separated himself from the others and was standing with the White woman who had been the translator.

"It's time to go," he whispered in Immanuel's ear. Give the man credit, he didn't turn or act surprised, it was like they had done this a thousand times. Immanuel whispered into the ear of the White woman translator, and she did turn and look at O'Bannon as if he were a specter in their midst.

They, all three, moved as a unit as the fireworks display continued overhead. Then there was a young boy who ran up to Immanuel and looked at him accusatorially.

Immanuel grabbed the boy, picking him up and

covering his mouth with his hand. The boy struggled, but it was a mere slip of a boy struggling against a man who weighed close to 275 pounds. They made it to the river, Immanuel found his horse, and the pack mule. The woman mounted a horse, she seemed to know what she was doing, and Immanuel and the boy were on his horse before Uzziah could even see him make the effort.

They rode downstream to where the black was tied up, and Uzziah was on the black and they were racing for the foothills not that far away.

All of a sudden, the night was deathly quiet. There wasn't a sound around except the thundering hooves of their horses and the mule as they made for the hills.

A cry went up from the village. Uzziah imagined they had discovered the missing White woman, Immanuel, and perhaps even the boy.

Uzziah rode up alongside Immanuel.

"Who's the boy?" he said as loudly as was permitted.

"The chief's son," Immanuel said.

"What!?" Uzziah said as if to ask the unspoken question.

Immanuel simply shrugged his shoulders.

It was then they heard a rider coming fast from behind. How could any of them have gotten to the horses, mounted up, and made it this close behind them? It was a puzzle.

Uzziah looked, and there the horse came, but without a rider! It was Samson, the plow horse mare who had followed them all the way from Fort Laramie. Uzziah pointed back at Immanuel, who had pulled a pistol from his boot and was aiming at the Apache who was catching up to them.

The two men smiled at each other when Immanuel saw it was Samson. Immanuel shook his head and laughed.

———

Apache were probably some of the best trackers among the Native American tribes. By sunup, they had discovered that Geronimo, the chief's son, was missing, and so was the White woman who had been among them for years and, obviously, the man, Immanuel, who had absconded with them. It took very little time for the tracking braves to find their trail. A war party of eighteen of the best braves was gathered together, and the chief was leading the party. After all, it was his son that they had taken!

———

Uzziah, Immanuel, the White woman, and Geronimo were well past the foothills by the time they stopped to eat. Uzziah stood guard on a huge boulder. He could see all the approaches to their position. The coffee smelled good, and Uzziah could hear Geronimo and the White woman talking Apache to each other.

"What's he saying?" Immanuel asked her.

"He says his father not far behind. It is believed in the village that this boy had the second sight and can see things which are happening far away."

"Well, ifn that's true, let's hope they're really far away," Immanuel joked, then thoughtfully, he confessed, "Hey, I didn't ask you ifn ya wanted to leave with us, that was kinda rude."

The White woman looked at Uzziah standing on the rock, back to Geronimo, then to Immanuel.

"I be with them since small child. Many moons have passed since I was taken. But when I see you," she said, looking at Immanuel. "I knew we'd be leaving together, if not this way, then another."

"So, you got the second sight, too?" Uzziah said from the rock.

"No, I was so surprised when I had feeling about him," she said and pointed to Immanuel.

"You got feelings for him?" Uzziah said, smiling at Immanuel, who gave Uzziah a dirty look.

"Yes," was all she said.

"Shh!" the boy shushed them and closed his eyes.

O'Bannon and Immanuel looked at each other and shrugged.

All of a sudden, a torrent of Apache came streaming from the boy's mouth. He was looking directly at the White woman, then as suddenly as he had started, he stopped and looked at the two White men.

"He says they closer than you think, must leave now, that his adventure with us will soon be over," she said, looking between the two mountain men.

"Well, let's skedaddle!" Immanuel said, throwing out what remained of the coffee Uzziah had made.

They mounted up immediately, and as Uzziah was getting on the black, an arrow whizzed by his head, and from below them, the Apache attacked.

Luckily for them, the weapons that shot lead possessed by the Apache were old and worn. Shots were fired, but all bullets veered wide of their marks, then again, maybe they were being careful not to shoot the chief's son.

As they galloped into the woods, Immanuel thought for the first time that maybe taking the chief's son had been a godsend. If things tanked toward an Apache victory, perhaps he could use the boy as a bargaining tool?!

7

When they finally stopped to actually rest, they must have ridden for twelve hours. The horses, except for the stallion, were played out. The White woman was asleep in the saddle, holding on to the night latch that Immanuel had pointed out to her.

There was another who did not seem tired from all the running, the boy, Geronimo. It seemed that this whole ordeal had been nothing more than an adventure in which the others were playing only a minor role.

That night, after one of Uzziah's suppers, the White woman and Immanuel had bedded down together. She was afraid to sleep in the mountains and said she was cold without another body near her. When she had voiced this, Immanuel and Uzziah looked at each other.

"You're the one who brought her along," Uzziah said, stating a truth and basically settling who would be spooning with her that night. They fell quickly to sleep, and the boy and Uzziah both chuckled when both started snoring.

"That one, the White woman, you could always tell which teepee she was in, those noises she makes, quite interesting," young Geronimo said.

Uzziah looked at him strangely. He hadn't heard the boy speak a word of English, and here he was, talking as if he had been born speaking the tongue.

"How do you know how to speak English?" Uzziah asked.

"I was once captured by the Comanches, and after two days, I spoke their language. My father, the chief, says I'm a natural mimic. Besides, she taught me. I asked her, and she could not refuse the son of the chief."

Just then, a snow owl called out in the night, and young Geronimo called back to it perfectly, just as if he were an owl.

"You will not be captured by my father and his braves."

"How do you know that?"

"I see into the future at times. Sometimes, I see great distances. For example, I knew you were looking at us through the long glass. Didn't you see me point at you?"

"I did."

"What more do you need. Geronimo has strong medicine, and you will not be captured by those who are in chase."

"Where are they now?" Uzziah asked.

"They are close, but also tired. They rest as we rest."

"How will we escape?"

"I will help you. My father plans on having me back

with him tomorrow, but if you do as I say, you will confound and astound him. I will help you on one condition."

"And that is?"

"Once you are away, and the White woman, we call her *Tears Out Hair*, but her English name is Jenny." He said the English name strangely. "She will stay with you. She has already thought of the one she lies with as her new husband."

"She has a husband within the tribe?"

"Oh yes, Terrible Man," Geronimo said.

"He beats her?"

"No, his name, Terrible Man," the boy said, thinking that Uzziah must be slow.

Uzziah looked over and smiled. *Careful who you take on an escape*, he thought to himself.

"So, kid, how do we avoid being captured by your father, the chief?"

"I will send him some confusing thoughts about where we are and what's happening to me," Geronimo said.

Uzziah looked at the boy, What was he, ten years old? All he could think about was how good the Apache were at tracking. Immanuel had already gone through that litany of their success in such endeavors. But would they, could they trust a boy with, essentially, the rest of their lives?

"Don't you want to know why I am helping you?"

"I give. Why are you helping us?"

"I am too often treated in the tribe as a boy. Yes, I am Geronimo, and the people know about my visions and powers, but still, they cannot get past my physical appearance. To them, Geronimo is just a boy, no matter how many times I show them my medicine. Besides, this is an adventure to me. I have heard about the mountain men and have met one. He died a good death, but I would like to know more, understand?"

Well, Uzziah sure understood the part about the only other mountain man the tribe had come into contact with had—how did he put it?—died a good death. A good death, a bad death, either way, you ended up dead, right?

——————

The next morning, Uzziah didn't sleep much. He was constantly waking up every time he heard anything. Well, hadn't the boy told him that the Apaches were close? He was so glad when Immanuel woke up.

"The kid says he can keep us from being caught," Uzziah said.

Immanuel looked at Uzziah like maybe he'd been hitting the bottle of whiskey he had in his saddlebags.

"So, how's this miracle goin' to take place?" Immanuel asked as he poured two cups of coffee, one for him and obviously another one for the woman.

"Her name is *Tears Out Hair*, or Jenny, whichever you prefer," Uzziah said to Immanuel.

"The boy tell you?"

"Yeah."

"Handy to know. Thanks," he said as he walked over and, kneeling down, offered her a cup of freedom.

"Well, how's he gonna do all that?" Immanuel said, walking back up to Uzziah, then looking down at the boy's blankets and him all curled up in them.

"Gonna send his pa, the chief, some confusing

thoughts," Uzziah said almost sheepishly. It sounded stupid now that he was telling his partner.

"Might work, he do have strong medicine," Immanuel said, and Uzziah was relieved that he didn't mock him.

Immanuel walked over and kicked the blankets and they were empty. Geronimo was gone! He looked at Uzziah, didn't say anything, then got the woman up, and all three of them were mounted up and pulling out when Geronimo ran into the camp. He jumped on Samson bareback, laughing.

"Let's go!" he said as he put his heels into Samson's sides.

"He speaks English?" Immanuel asked, looking at Uzziah.

"Yeah, he does," was all Uzziah could say.

"Where were you, boy?" Immanuel growled.

"Even a boy must relieve himself."

———

If the young Geronimo was sending the chief, his father, some confusing thoughts, they must also have been sent to the two White men's brains. They could not for the life of them figure out what the boy was doing. He'd ride south for half an hour, then go east for half an hour, then west for an hour. If Immanuel hadn't been in the mountains for as long as he had, he probably would have gotten turned around.

"Where the hell are we goin'?" Uzziah asked Immanuel.

"Ask the boy, he's either crazy or the best track breaker I've ever seen."

They traveled on like that, in that peculiar manner, for the rest of the day. Immanuel figured they were about four miles from their breakfast camp that morning. As they settled down, he took a ride around to see if he could find any sign of the chief and his braves. When he got back to camp, Geronimo was fixing fry bread for them, and Uzziah had shot with his bow a couple of squirrels. Squirrel and fry bread, it was.

"Couldn't find any sign of them, could you?" Geronimo asked, eating his second helping of fry bread.

"No, where are they?" Immanuel asked.

"They have gone back to the plains. My father thinks you have doubled back to avoid him."

"How he get that idea?" Uzziah asked.

"I sent him those thoughts. At first, he resisted, but then he could not."

"Where are they now?" Immanuel asked.

"Still camping on the plains. They have gone back to the village to consult the medicine man and get resupplied."

"Then, I'd like to go to where we will ride out the winter, if that's okay with you?" he was asking Geronimo's permission to travel on.

"Will you go without me?"

"We'd really like to not show you where we will be all winter," Immanuel said.

"The Apache will not go into the mountains once the first big snow comes. Please allow me to be with you a while longer. I am learning many things."

Immanuel talked it over with Uzziah and they both agreed. The boy could go to their camp, but he'd have to be blindfolded, and sat backward on his horse, and led in. When it came time for him to leave, he would be led out in the same manner. All that was left was convincing the boy of their plan.

————

He fought like a wildcat. He was not onboard with the plan and started to scream, which meant they had to gag as well as blindfold the boy. When they put him on the horse backward, he knew immediately, but was so disoriented by the time they started out that he finally fell into a silence which was foreboding.

Uzziah was certain that he was going to send his father, the chief, their exact location and how to find them. All he could hope for was that the blindfold, sitting backward on the horse, and not being able to talk would throw off his medicine.

But even though they traveled like that for the entire day, the boy did not make another peep. He was offered water when they stopped at clear mountain streams. He was handed jerky and hard tack, which he threw away. It seemed as if he would never forgive them for what they were doing.

They took off the gag and blindfold when they stopped for the night. He would not look at any of them. When they asked him a question, he was silent. Finally, Jenny, Tears Out Hair, talked quietly with him in Apache, and as she was talking, his eyes wandered over to the men. He gave them hard looks, but both Immanuel and Uzziah were adult men, they had been looked at harshly before.

At supper, with everyone around the fire, and the rabbits which Uzziah had shot with this bow, were being devoured, and the biscuits eaten, the boy spoke.

"I have never been treated with such disrespect. My anger kept me from sending for my father. Being backward on the horse also made the journey feel like sickness. But now that I am on the earth without restraints, my anger has gone. If you must know, as the only son of the chief, I have not been allowed to do much with my people. Their fear of my being hurt or killed has kept me from most hunts, and whenever the braves go out to count coup, I am not with them. I ask only one thing of you two men," he said and looked at them gravely.

"Uzziah and I would never hurt a boy, no matter where he comes from. We took you, well, I took you as a ransom against getting caught again. My fear overcame my better judgment."

"What do you want, son?" Uzziah simply asked.

Geronimo looked away from Immanuel and toward Uzziah, who got the definite impression he was about to be told what the boy wanted.

"I want you to teach me how to live in these most harsh conditions, to hunt in them, to shelter down when the snow comes, and when I have learned enough, I will leave."

"My fear is that when you leave, you will bring back Apache, who will do us harm," Immanuel admitted.

"I could, if I wanted to, but teaching me these things which are out of the range of knowledge of most Apache, will make me a better leader when my time comes. Don't you see, if I can lead my people into these frozen mountains and actually survive, can you imagine how we would confound the cavalry of the Army? They know us as a desert people and only as desert people. Will you do this for me?"

Uzziah and Immanuel walked away from the fire

into the darkness of the night. They looked back and could see the boy eating more rabbit and he and Jenny talking amicably in Apache.

"What do you think, partner?" Immanuel asked, looking back toward the warm glow of their fire.

"I think we'd be playing with fire, that's what I think," Uzziah said, looking back at the same scene.

"You mean if he's full of shite, and his old man, the chief, just showed up."

"Something like that. Why don't we just let him go, and he can take Samson."

"I thought you liked that old mare," Immanuel asked.

"I do, but bringing the boy with us, taking him even further away from his tribe. I don't think it's a good idea," Uzziah said, sorry really, because on some level, he thought it might be interesting to get to know this kid, who would be a future Apache leader.

"Yeah, you're right. Besides, now that he don't want us to blindfold him. We can't exactly lead him to where we're gonna be livin'!"

When they both walked back to the fire, the young boy had been basically put to bed by Jenny. Immanuel snuggled in with Jenny, and Uzziah rolled up in his blankets close to the fire. It looked earlier, when the sun was going down, like it might snow, but they would be at the cabins tomorrow.

———

When they got up the next morning, there was a skiff of snow, well, about two inches, which Immanuel considered a skiff, but which Uzziah thought was a lot. The boy, Geronimo, was gone. So was the mare, Samson.

"Where do ya think he went?" Uzziah asked Immanuel.

"I have no idea," Immanuel said, then he turned to Jenny. "Did the boy stay with you the entire time Uzziah and I were away from the fire last night?"

"Almost," she said.

"What's that mean, almost?"

"He said he had to relieve himself, and he was gone for a bit," she said.

"He heard us talking," Uzziah said.

"He even took the horse we wanted him to take."

"What you two talking about?" Jenny wanted to know.

"We was planning on sending him back to his pa, the chief, even though he wanted otherwise."

"He's a proud boy. Probably took off to avoid being sent off," Uzziah offered.

"Which reminds me, if he's holding it against us that we didn't want him along, we'd better make some tracks and not bother with breakfast. Pack up and let's go!" Immanuel said, thinking that the last thing he wanted was to tangle with a bunch of braves led by Geronimo's father.

———

They lit out of there within the half hour. They traveled long and hard and made it to the cabins before it was dark. The meat that they'd hung from the trees before they took off to get the cache was scavenged by bears, cougars, and whatever animals could get to it. They would have to hunt again, and soon.

Immanuel and Jenny settled into the cabin farthest away from Uzziah's south-facing cabin. He liked that idea because he had awakened several times since they left the Apache village and heard their moaning. Not that it bothered him, but it did bother him. Since he had no woman, it was better for him not to think about the comforts and the warmth that a woman could bring a man.

That night, when the three of them said good night and Uzziah went into his own cabin, he was mighty glad that the potbellied stove was fired up and the cabin he'd sleep in was going to be warm and toasty.

He fell asleep almost immediately. He hadn't felt safe since Immanuel had been captured by the Apache, and letting his mind go of any troubles that they might be facing, he thought about going out and checking the traps, which were long overdue.

8

Uzziah volunteered the next morning to go and check all the traps. Immanuel was reluctant to let him do that, but Jenny had been asking him to make some changes in the cabin they were staying in, and to both Immanuel and Uzziah, it seemed a good time for him to disappear for a day.

As Uzziah had mounted up and was ready to ride out on the black, Immanuel came out.

"Hey, partner, I hope ya don't feel like you're gettin' stuck with this duty?"

"Nah, I don't. It has to be done."

"Make sure to secure the traps, or we'll end up with traps all over the ponds. And if there are any drowned beaver from being caught, just toss 'em in the bush, something will eat 'em."

Uzziah rode off. He had his own thoughts to occupy his mind. He'd never been a person who dwelled on the negative side of anything. Sure, he'd thought that he and Immanuel would be up here on their lonesome, but having a squaw around, even if she was White, would alleviate a lot of the work. The hides could be scraped and cured by her. She could make the hook rings out of willow branches that they would stretch the hides on. And, most of all, from what he'd tasted on the trail, she was a better cook than either one of them.

He worked the better part of the morning till afternoon. His thoughts occupied his mind, and unlike a seasoned mountain man, he wasn't paying a whole lot of attention to his surroundings. Later, he was sure that was the only way what happened to him could have happened.

He was at the last pond where they'd set traps and was surprised he'd gotten done as much work as he had. When he'd started out that morning, he was fairly sure that it would take him the better part of two days to do the work, but even though the sun was getting lower, he was almost done!

So, when he looked up after setting a trap, the last one, he was surprised to see Geronimo sitting on Samson.

"Well, hello there," Uzziah said trying not to act too surprised.

"I have been following you for hours, and it is only when I ride into view that you notice I'm here?"

"Well, you are an Apache, and I am a White man," Uzziah said, chuckling to himself.

"True, it is only in your numbers that you are greater. In every other way, the White man is inferior to the Apache."

"So, you didn't go back to your people?"

"I started out to. I overheard what you and Immanuel were going to do, so I did it myself. I was so mad that you didn't want to teach me, I swore an oath

I'd get the braves, come back, scalp both of you, and rescue Tears Out Hair."

"And what changed your mind?"

"I couldn't find them. I guess they continued to follow the buffalo, and it seems the buffalo went south, and so did the Apache."

"You found us up here, but you couldn't track them south?" Uzziah wasn't sure what this young boy was thinking.

"I am not used to people not doing what I want. I am the son of a chief and someday will be the most important chief to ever live among my people. I have had a vision that, in the far future, White men, soldiers, will jump from metal birds to their deaths screaming my name!"

"I don't know if you should put much credence into those visions of yours."

"Regardless, I am here now, and I have been watching very carefully what you've been doing. It is not hard work. Is this all a mountain man does?"

"Funny thing about that. I came up here to learn the mountain ways from Immanuel. I ain't really a true mountain man yet."

"Then why am I watching you!? Let's go and learn the mountain ways from the real mountain man, Immanuel."

Uzziah mounted back up and let Geronimo take the lead just to see if he really did know the way to the cabins. He did. When they showed up there, it was twilight. As they rode in, Immanuel came out. He and Jenny both did a double-take when they saw the young Apache boy.

"You'd thought you'd seen the last of me, didn't ya?" Geronimo said.

———

Once it had been discovered that Geronimo hadn't gone back to his tribe and there weren't a bunch of Injuns coming up the trail to decimate them, Immanuel settled down. Jenny was glad to see the boy because he had always been good to her, even when most of the Apache women treated her with disdain. The two of them, familiar with each other, had fallen into talking Apache with one another and making dinner.

Immanuel and Uzziah went to his cabin, where Uzziah built back the fire in his potbellied stove, and the two men sat there and smoked.

"And you think that's all he wants?" Immanuel asked Uzziah.

"Seems that way. I mean, if he trailed us back up here, he could have found the tribe. The boy is fascinated by White men living in the mountains, and he wants to learn our, I mean, your ways."

"So now, instead of just having to break in a partner, which, by the way, I've never had, I got to teach a snot-nosed kid what we're up to. Do you have any idea how much that goes against my nature!?"

"Can I mention something that's fairly obvious?" Uzziah asked, sending his eyes back into the other cabin where Jenny and Geronimo were chatting away in Apache.

"Yeah, about that, what can I say?"

"I'm okay with her being up here. I'm sure she's not the first or last squaw ya had livin' up heres."

"She's not, but she is the first White woman. Keep thinking back to what we said to Billy back at Fort Laramie, 'Ya ever heard of any mountain women?'"

"Yeah, that one's comin' back to haunt us, ain't it?"

"So, what do you think we should do?" Immanuel asked.

"Teach the boy. He's eager to learn. It's not like he's gonna be any competition. As soon as he figures out he's learned what he can, then he'll leave."

"You don't understand, partner. It's about to get hairy with snow up this way. It'll take me a month to teach him, then we won't be able to get outta the mountains, come hell or high water!"

"He's like a bad penny, he ain't goin' away," Uzziah said. "I truly don't know what to do."

"Well, we got a couple weeks probably before it'll be too much snow to get out. There's only one thing we can do. We got to get the boy back to his pa, and his pa done fawllered the buffs south. We trap along the ridges from here to almost the Mexican border. So, we leave Jenny here and trap our way south until we get to where, if we left the Rockies, we'd be in Apache territory. Then we take the boy home."

"Sounds like a plan, but what do ya think Jenny and the boy will say?"

———

They had a lot to say. Mostly, at first, it was Jenny. She wasn't about to be left in those cabins by herself for as long as it would take them to take the boy home by trapping the Rockies down to the Arizona territories. She was going, and that was that.

The boy, Geronimo, thought it was the best of all possible solutions to both their problems. He wanted to learn the mountain man ways, and they wanted him to be back with his people.

The next day, it took them almost the entire day to pack for the coming trip. They loaded down the pack mule and took as many items on their persons as they could. Geronimo would ride Samson, Jenny would ride one of the other horses which basically they had stolen when they escaped the Apache village, and everyone would have a mount. As it turned out, she stole the very horse that she rode when she was with them, so everyone was happy.

They rode south, stopping along streams and ponds and setting their traps at night. The following evening, they'd check the traps for beaver, grab up what they'd caught, and Jenny and the boy would clean the pelts and at least make them suitable for taking with them. The fact that the weather was so cold that the pelts froze was actually good. The frozen pelts could be taken to the Apache village and cured there. At least that's what Immanuel hoped.

It turned out Geronimo wanted more than anything to learn to shoot the long rifles that both Uzziah and Immanuel carried. The Hawken is a powerful weapon, and they decided to teach him to shoot it lying down. That way, he'd already be on the ground instead of being thrown to it.

One afternoon, after setting traps, they went hunting. Geronimo had seen tracks of some elk and they followed them down into a swale where the animals were watering at a stream.

"Now, the wind's comin' from the herd, not us. That's good—"

"'Cause they can't smell us, right?"

"Are ya teachin' me, or am I teachin' you?" Immanuel asked the boy.

"Sorry, go ahead."

"You gonna lay down in those deerskin clothes that Jenny made you and sight in on the buck down there. Ya see the one I mean?"

"The big one, right?"

"Right, now pulling this trigger may pull the gun off the target, so ya gotta be very careful to squeeze slow like. Okay?"

Geronimo lay down with the weapon. They had cut a fork from a tree branch, driven it into the ground, and laid the barrel in the Y it made. There was little chance that the boy would miss if he followed Immanuel's instructions.

He sighted in for an incredibly long time, and the big buck elk kept moving, which meant he had to move the Hawken to sight in again.

"Could ya do this while we're still young?" Immanuel asked him.

"Impossible, that was before I was born," Geronimo said. Then, when they were least expecting it, he pulled the trigger.

Both men jumped as if they had been shot, and down range, the big bull elk reared up on its hind legs and fell over dead.

———

They had to get Samson down in the ravine to carry the bull elk out, and that night, they had elk steaks.

Truth be told, Immanuel and Uzziah were learning just about as much as the young boy, Geronimo. It seemed he had an extensive knowledge of plants, barks, and other remedies that even Immanuel had never heard of.

They had been lucky. The winter that hit them, when it did hit them, was not as bad as in years before. It was almost as if the really bad weather was waiting for the new year, which wasn't that unusual.

By the time they had made it far enough south to come out of the mountains and into the territories that would eventually lead into Mexico, it had been almost six weeks since Geronimo had seen his relatives or his tribe. The boy was excited the night before they were to ride into the camp. He had cleaned up the deerskin outfit that Jenny had made him, greased his long hair up, and made a band around his head in which he placed two eagle feathers.

"He's treating this like it was a vision quest or something," Immanuel said to Uzziah.

"How so?"

"Well, look at him! He wants to go back to his people looking and even sounding different. No doubt, he will try his new English out on them, and God knows what else."

"Why can't we just let him go into the village by himself?" Uzziah wanted to know.

"Don't you get it? He wants to come back to his father, the chief, with the very men who stole him from the tribe up north."

"But won't they want some sort of retribution for the boy being with us?"

"Who knows. We got ourselves into this, and my guess is, we can get ourselves out. The pelts will help. There's a lot of money in all those pelts, and beaver ain't exactly the fur of choice in the desert."

———————

The morning they rode toward the Apache village, it was cold, and the wind was blowing toward the mountains. They looked like just what they were—two mountain men, a squaw, and a younger Injun. Except, the way he was dressed was not a traditional look for the Apache, and once they were sighted, things were bound to get interesting.

It was one of the young boys who was watching the horses down by the creek who first saw them. He left his companion to continue watching and ran toward the village, an alarm in his voice. Soon, several dozen braves were mounted and riding post-haste toward the band of four who were riding toward their village. They would count coup, take prisoners, and anything of value that the four had on them.

The chief had decided to go with the war party, for he had been despondent lately over the loss of his only son, Geronimo. The boy had been seen by most of the Apache people as a good omen, that's why he had been treated with kid gloves and such deference.

Immanuel saw them coming at a gallop and turned to the other three.

"We are not gonna run, nor are we gonna act scared

at all. After all, we got the prize and they don't even know it."

It seemed Geronimo puffed out his ten-year-old chest a bit more when he heard those words and rode taller on Samson.

They began to hear the screaming of the Apache, which was always meant to scare the bejesus out of those they attacked. Uzziah was not exactly sure what would happen, and in the moments before they were overrun, he said a silent prayer to his creator.

———

There was something about the way the four rode that clued Geronimo's pa into thinking there was more to these four riders than met the eye. He had had a consistent and very annoying dream in which he found his son but was always awakened shortly before they could embrace. The dream was driving him crazy, and his medicine man could not come up with a sufficient explanation for it. Now, as the chief rode closer, and was beginning to get a better look at all four riders, he realized one of them was riding bareback and used a rope halter which was made and used by all Apache.

———

As the dozen braves surrounded the four riders, and as they, the four, came to a halt, everyone knew something special was happening. The yelling stopped, and the mood was one of contemplation, not coup.

Jenny was the first to speak. She spoke in Apache to

them all, but she was looking at the chief the entire time, and this is what she heard back to her in Apache.

"Has my son returned with his captors to have them punished?"

Much to Jenny and the chief's surprise, Geronimo answered in English, and she translated.

"No, Father," he said in his English tongue. "I have come with many pelts of beaver and with the hind quarter of a bull elk, which I shot with the White man's long gun. I have learned the ways of the mountain men, and when our tribe is threatened by the Whites, as surely they must be, it will be I, Geronimo, who shall lead them safely into the mountains where we can continue to be a tribe."

As he was speaking, all the Apache looked around at those with them as if to ask, *How is this possible?*

Jenny translated Geronimo's words, and the effect it had on the braves there was nothing short of amazing. They seemed to know that the boy who had left them, albeit under duress, was returning to them a different sort of boy, a man/boy, if you will. A boy who had been taken but turned the tables on his captors, getting them to bend to his will, teach him the mountain ways, and now, returning in triumph to his people. It all seemed to be going too well, then one brave rode out from the back of the pack.

Jenny sucked in her breath and cowered in the saddle.

"This my Apache husband, Terrible Man," she said.

By this time, the chief, glad to finally have the dream in which he did not get his son back, revealed to be a dream about getting him back, but now different, was speaking to Jenny, who could not take her eyes off Terrible Man.

"The chief says we all must come to the village and we will have a celebration, but before we celebrate, you and Terrible Man must fight to the death to see who I belong to," Jenny said.

"Great, to the death, ya say?" Immanuel said. "Well, there ain't no gain without a risk. How do you feel about Terrible Man?" he asked Jenny, sure the others wouldn't know what he was saying.

"He is a brave warrior, but my heart is now yours, Immanuel."

"That's sorta what I thought."

Geronimo rode next to his father back to the village. The chief kept reaching over and touching his son, making sure this wasn't part of the same dream he'd been having. By the time they got close enough, the ululation of the women filled the air, and every single soul there knew that something was happening.

9

The women had already begun fixing some of the tantalizing foods that were to be a part of the celebration. The king's son had returned, the prodigal had returned. The fattened calf would be killed, the robe, ring, and sandals would all be his. But first, there had to be a fight to the death over a woman. Somehow, Uzziah didn't remember that part of the prodigal story.

Immanuel had stripped down to nothing but his deerskin breeches. His body had been rubbed with bear fat so that it would be harder for his opponent, Terrible Man, to grab him and knife him through. It was like a duel that Uzziah had read about in a book back in Virginia. He was there with Immanuel, and across the way, several braves were attending to Terrible Man. He, too, was stripped to the waist, but with only a loincloth on. The knife he was passing back and forth between his massive hands looked more like a sword.

"How come your knife ain't as big as his?" Uzziah asked Immanuel.

"Good damn question. I ain't ever seen a knife that big."

"What's yer strategy?"

"Not to get kilt," Immanuel said, and there was a loud gunshot, which neither of them expected, and it seemed the match to the death was on.

Both men circled each other, both making stabbing motions toward the other. Immanuel was as big as Terrible Man, but the look in the Apache's eyes told the tale of a wronged husband, and truthfully, Uzziah started planning how he was going to escape when Immanuel was impaled. What could he do? Yes, he still had his Hawken and his pistols, but even if every shot he fired killed someone, there would be enough enemies left over to do him in, that was for sure.

Terrible Man lunged at Immanuel and cut him across the stomach. It wasn't deep, but soon, the deer-skin breeches were soaked in blood all the way to his bare feet. How much blood could the big man lose before he got woozy?

Immanuel feigned being hurt worse than he was, and Terrible Man lunged at him again, but this time, a handful of dirt, which Immanuel must have gathered up when he bowed low with the cut, was thrown into Terrible Man's eyes.

The Apache liked that, and the braves ululated along with the women. Terrible Man was swiping left and right and all around, afraid that Immanuel would move in for the kill. Jenny threw him his shirt, which he wound around his body, staunching the flow of blood. Now he was ready again. Terrible Man's eyes had caught the help from Jenny, and it was obvious he didn't like it.

Terrible Man screamed a blood-curdling scream and, taking the knife by the enormous blade, he flung it at Immanuel, who successfully ducked by throwing himself into the dirt flat on his stomach.

There was a groan from the crowd encircling the fighters. The knife had found a place to lodge, but unfortunately, it was in Jenny's stomach. She went down hard, and both men ran to her side.

———

The rest of the day saw both men attending to Jenny in Terrible Man's teepee. She was badly wounded, and Immanuel did what he could to staunch the bleeding and patch her up. Terrible Man had the medicine man in there, drumming, chanting, and dancing all around, quite to the annoyance of Immanuel. Uzziah was in there, too, because he was afraid of what would happen when Jenny died, which he was sure she would.

The woman has roused herself and pulled Terrible Man to her. She was whispering in Apache. Uzziah could hear, but he could not understand. Immanuel was sitting back on his knees on the other side of her, but she held to Terrible Man and kept whispering, whispering. Terrible Man broke down in tears, but the torrent of whispers continued in Apache. Immanuel almost felt sorry for the man. Then, she let go of Terrible Man and latched onto Immanuel.

"My darling, I must tell you how you brought back my heritage, my beginnings to me, how much I love you for doing that. You took me back to the language of my parents, and yes, it was painful to see again the way they were murdered, the manner in which my brothers' heads were dashed against the wagon wheels, the scalping of all my kin. But trying to forget all that, I forgot the love with which they had raised me, my brothers' teasing ways, and how much I was loved in the middle of that family. I should have died many years ago, and after being brought here, if it hadn't been for Terrible Man, I would have died from lack of attention. Promise me, if you have any feelings for me at all, you and Terrible Man must make peace now. You are the only two men I have ever loved."

"Oh Jenny, I thought we would be together in the mountains I love. You are the perfect woman for me, squaw, but not squaw. Your flaxen hair will haunt me for the rest of my life. I am so sorry to have anything to do with your death. If I knew this would have happened, I would have let him kill me and be done with it," Immanuel said, holding her head to his chest and weeping, but his words were lost on the woman in his arms. She had passed with loving words being spoken over her, and who among us would not wish such a death?

Uzziah stepped out of the tent as Immanuel was speaking to Jenny. He had to get some fresh air. There was the smell of death in Terrible Man's teepee.

"Will she live?" It was Geronimo.

"Probably not," Uzziah said, then added, "What will happen if she doesn't live?"

"Have you noticed the celebration for my return has gone on in spite of Jenny's dying?"

"Yeah, it's like they don't really care," Uzziah said, looking around at all the people eating, dancing, and celebrating.

"They don't."

"Why not?"

"She was captured when she was younger than I am now, just seven years old. They expected her to be a slave to one of the chief's wives. She was treated badly until Terrible Man saw her being beaten one day. He took her under his wing, she was almost sixteen then. No one dared touch her, and in another year, he married her."

"Do they have children?"

"No, it was seen as a punishment against Terrible Man for him taking the side of a White over his own people."

"But he stayed with her?"

"He took other wives, they gave him children, but he could not let go of Tears Out Hair."

"There are some women who affect men like that," Uzziah said.

"I hope I never find one like that."

"Why?" Uzziah asked, turning toward the boy.

"Because whoever might kill the one like that which I loved, I would spend the rest of my life killing them and theirs."

"Maybe it would be worth it, just to love like that," Uzziah suggested.

"I hope not," Geronimo said.

Uzziah watched as Immanuel walked from the teepee of Terrible Man. He picked up his Hawken rifle and fired it into the air.

"She has died," Geronimo said, and he reached up and tore off his deerskin shirt and then his pants, which left him standing in just his breechcloth.

Much to Uzziah's surprise, everyone had stopped celebrating and were tearing their clothes and wailing.

Terrible Man walked from the teepee and called to his other wives. They entered the teepee.

"They will clean the body, wash her beautiful blond hair, and prepare her for burial," Geronimo explained.

Immanuel had torn off all his clothes and was standing next to Terrible Man, who had done the same. Both naked men walked to the large fire, which, moments before, braves had been dancing around.

Terrible Man held the bone of a horse close to the fire and, when it was red hot, burned his hair to shoulder length. He offered the bone to Immanuel, who did precisely the same thing.

"The death of this woman may save everyone," Geronimo whispered to Uzziah.

"What do you mean?"

"I have heard the story of your God's son, how he came and died, and that death saved everyone from death. So, it is with the one who has died here today."

"Poor Jenny," Uzziah said.

Geronimo put his hand over Uzziah's mouth.

"Once the dead have left, we do not speak their names." Uzziah's heart skipped a beat as he remembered the first time he'd heard that, when Immanuel had stopped him from saying Sarah's name. Now, they both had lost women to the cruelties of this world.

———

Jenny's body was brought out and laid near the fire, where Terrible Man's wives worked on her. She was dressed in the best dress that was available in the tribe. Pollen was sprinkled on her face, and her hair entwined with dried flowers. When all the preparations had been made, they turned to Terrible Man and handed him the bowl of pollen. He turned to Immanuel, who, hours before, had been his mortal enemy. They walked over to the body, those two naked men, and bending down, Terrible Man dipped his index finger into the pollen and drew a straight line across her forehead, right above the eyes and nose. He handed the bowl to Immanuel, whose tears were silently making their way down his chest.

Dipping his finger into the pollen, he drew an intersecting line down from the hairline through the horizontal line, stopping right before the nose. She was now wearing a pollen cross, or the sign of the four directions.

The sun was still up, so they walked, the entire tribe, to a section of rocks that were in the foothills a couple of miles away. They had Jenny wrapped in fine cloth, which someone had brought to them. The two men carried her. Her head by Terrible Man's chest and her legs across the arms of Immanuel.

They found a cleft in the rocks and placed her body in it. Other rocks surrounding the cleft were pushed into the space between the rocks until the cleft was sealed. Prayers were said. Uzziah did not understand the Apache prayers, but above them, he could hear Immanuel singing, *Holy, holy, holy, Lord God Almighty*. His voice was so clear, it carried so well in the twilight air, that soon, all the other prayers and attempts at mourning ceased, and like a clarion call, the words rang out.

"*Holy, Holy, Holy, Lord God Almighty. Early in the morning, our song shall rise to Thee. Holy, Holy, Holy, Merciful and Mighty, God in three persons. Blessed*

Trinity. Holy, Holy, Holy. All the saints adore Thee. Casting down their golden crowns around the glassy sea. Cherubim and seraphim falling down before Thee. Which wert and art, and evermore shalt be."

Terrible Man held out his arm to Immanuel when the song was finished and they clasped forearms, a sign of true friendship.

EPILOGUE

The next morning, Uzziah and Immanuel rode from the village. Geronimo rode with them to the foothills, where he reined in Samson. He looked lost up on the plow horse's back, a child riding a behemoth. They rode three abreast until they came to the foothills, then they reined in alongside Geronimo.

The three of them looked at each other like they were all waiting for someone to say something.

"You have taught me well," Geronimo said, "and I shall never forget."

"Well, son," Immanuel started in, "you're just about the last person I will forget."

"The death of the one who died was unfortunate, but as I mentioned to your partner, her death released both of you."

"I don't know why, but last night I had a dream," began Uzziah, "and I don't normally put much stock in such things, but I have to tell you what I saw."

"Please do, the Apache put much stock in dreams."

"You were an old man, but still the chief of your

people. Your nation was the last nation to continue to fight against the whites."

"Ah, this is a good dream," Geronimo said as he leaned against the neck of Samson.

"Here's the weird part. People were driving around in carriages which were not being pulled by horses."

"What did they look like?" Immanuel asked.

"The people or the carriages?"

"Both," Immanuel was interested.

"The people looked the same as we do now. They had cowboy hats on and wore guns, but the carriages had smoke coming from the back of them."

"They were on fire?" Geronimo asked.

"No, the smoke only came when the carriages moved. Very strange, don't you think?"

"So, when I am old and I see people in carriages which are not pulled by the cayuse, then I will still be fighting the whites."

"Well, you were in my dream," Uzziah said.

Geronimo rode up beside Uzziah's horse and, reaching across, grabbed his forearm.

"You've taught me, and now you gift me with this dream. I shall never stop fighting until I see these carriages with no horses."

"Well, ifn we're to git along, we'd better git along," Immanuel said, anxious to put miles behind them.

They rode off from the young boy, who would someday become the chief of the Bedonkohe band of Chiricahua Apaches. They had no idea just how powerful Geronimo would become, nor how his first wife and children would be killed by the Mexican Federales and how, for the rest of his life, he would go out of his way to murder and maim those same kinds of soldiers. And finally, in 1923, when Geronimo was captured by the US Marshals, he saw riding around him the carriages without horses. They called them automobiles, and he was smiling when they led him to captivity. The mountain man Uzziah O'Bannon had been right. He fought until he was old, and it was the Apache who would always be remembered as the last of the tribes to fight for what they knew was right.

But none of the three men, well, one was just a boy, had any idea about the future. O'Bannon and Jones were headed back to their mountains, and it was their mountains now. They had started out for an easy ride into the Rockies, and then, things changed. There was an old saying, *Men make plans, and God laughs*. Their plans now were to return to the cabins and live peacefully and without trouble amid the beauty of those same mountains, but if they had listened well, they could have heard the chuckling of the Lord.

MAD ENOUGH TO KILL

1

Uzziah O'Bannon and Immanuel James Jones had made it through their first year as partners. They had only had one serious fight, where they resorted to long knives, but that fight, after it had spilled into the early spring snow, was interrupted by a sleepy grizzly bear who got on his hind legs and growled something fierce at them. They both turned from fighting one another to throwing their knives into the griz, which only made him madder than hell. Hawken rifles were grabbed, and the big sleepy monster was finished off. They had bear steaks that night and laughed about how the fight had got them mad enough to kill and it was a good thing something came along that needed killing.

Immanuel had missed Rendezvous the year before and he swore he'd never miss another. They left early in summer to be able to go by Fort Laramie. Immanuel said the whiskey the purveyors brought to the rendezvous always gave him a terrible headache and they were going to get decent whiskey at Fort Laramie then go on from there.

Both the men's beards had grown considerably and Uzziah kept teasing Immanuel about all the gray in his beard.

"I'm just gonna hafta start callin' ya Father Christmas, that's what I'm gonna do," Uzziah teased his partner.

"Yeah, well, yer gonna get nothin' but coal in yer stockin' this year, old son," Immanuel quipped back.

They had made it within a day's ride to the fort and both men were anxious to see, among other things, women!

That night, Immanuel had a dream. He pretended he didn't put much stock in dreams, but the truth was, his were so graphic and real that when he was dreaming, he thought he was actually doing what he was doing. Sometimes, that set up a sort of situation in which he found himself in those exact circumstances. Once, he'd dreamed he'd almost been scalped by a Blackfoot Injun, and the next day he almost was!

In the dream, he was a younger man, and he liked that. He was in charge of a bunch of wagons and as far as he could tell by the way people were treating him in the dream, he must have been some kind of leader. A wagon master, maybe? He'd never wanted any sort of job like that, people depending on you to get them somewhere and you responsible for their lives?! It was hard enough in this life to keep your own life and livelihood.

In the dream, he'd circled the wagons, and they were fighting the Apache of all people. He saw Geronimo as an adult, and he tied a white bandana onto his Hawken and rode out to have a parley with the great chief. He thought that since he'd taught Geronimo about the mountains and how to trap and all, this bloodshed could be avoided if he only talked to the chief.

When he rode out with the white flag, the Apache stopped circling the wagons and gathered around their chief.

"How! Geronimo, you remember me?" Immanuel said, and the chief just lowered his rifle and shot a big hole in Immanuel's chest. Guess that was one answer.

When he woke, it was only false dawn, so he got up and made breakfast. The thought of being killed by a kid who had grown up and then turned on him rankled the old mountain man.

Uzziah got up and grunted as he walked away from their camp, and the long stream of piss which came from his body was so continuous Immanuel had to say something.

"How can anybody have that much piss in 'em?"

"Considering the fact that you get up about as many times as the stage stops between Denver and Lincoln, I'd say it's better to save it till mornin'," Uzziah quipped.

"It's either that or piss the bedroll," Immanuel said, slamming the bacon over like it had insulted him.

"Well, now nature's tellin' me I got to finish with a grunt," Uzziah said, and walking off further behind some rocks, he pulled down his trousers and did his business.

"I am one happy nigger that the wind is blowing toward you so I don't hafta smell your shite."

Uzziah came walking back into the camp and sighed.

"Now, I'm good for the rest of the day."

"Uh-huh, have some of this, and we'll get goin'. I can taste that bonded whiskey now."

"And you got cash money to pay for it?"

"My God, old son, haven't ya learned nothin', ya trade fer things, trade fer things, a few pelts outta get us some fine, not headache-making whiskey. Ya don't have to thank me, ya smelly old goat—my God, the wind has changed directions and yer shite smell is waftin' this way!" he complained.

They rode for the entire day without dismounting. Well, the usual stops for watering the horses, and relieving oneself. When the fort came into view, Uzziah kicked the black stallion up and Immanuel simply grunted, he wasn't about to race to the fort.

The man guarding the gate saw Uzziah racing toward the gate, and he hollered out a warning.

"Rider comin' fast!" was all he said, but that interested all the guards since they spent the better part of every day simply going blind, staring at nothing. Some rifles were aimed at Immanuel since they thought the one coming in fast might be pursued by a bad hombre. And yet, the man riding behind the fast rider was poking along so slowly that they simply opened the gate to let the fast rider on the sleek black horse into the fort.

Uzziah came in with a flourish and, pulling back on the reins, skidded the black horse to a stop. Dust shot up around him and there were complaints from some of those standing around.

"What's the meaning of this, sir?" asked an officer who just happened to be on his way to the commissary.

"Sorry," Uzziah lied, "sometimes old blackie just don't like to walk."

The officer came closer and inspected the horse.

"Why that's a fine animal, I don't suppose ya'd sell him, would ya?"

"Not for all the money in Fort Laramie."

"Harrumph," the officer said as Immanuel sauntered into the middle of the parade area.

"You make a nuisance of yerself already?"

"Almost made us a passel of greens," Uzziah bragged.

"Let me guess, the officer wanted yer horse?"

"How'd ya know?"

"What else ya got that's worth anything?"

A cry came from the guard at the gate. "Riderless horse comin' in!"

"There's our pelts, now!" Uzziah said.

When the gate was opened, Samson, heavy-laden with cured pelts, came walking into the fort. He caused quite a stir. Soldiers were standing around asking how this horse was out traveling by himself, and all sorts of speculations were going around.

"He's ours!" Immanuel shouted at them, and Samson came walking over and stood between the two mountain men's horses.

Samson had been given to Geronimo at the beginning of last winter, but the horse came wandering back up to the cabins after a few days. Either Geronimo the boy had let him go or he simply followed the two men like a faithful dog. They didn't complain, the horse was strong as an ox and never needed to be tethered. He came along at his own pace, and the pelts were safe. If anyone had approached Samson out on the plains, he would have kicked it into a higher gear and found the two men.

It was about then that both men's ears were

accosted by the scream of a girl and the yelling of a boy. When they turned in the saddle and looked, there came Billy Patterson and his sister, Karen. Both men thought it was amazing how the two children had grown up over the winter. They looked like the same kids, but Billy looked a whole heap older, like maybe he was a junior man or something. Karen had changed in a different way. She looked like the shrunken image of a lady. Her blond hair was combed nicely, and both kids looked like the people from the other wagons had sort of adopted them and things were good.

"You've come back fer us!" Billy yelled at the top of his lungs. "I told 'em ya'd be back, but they laughed at me, sayin' no two men were ever as glad to get rid of two kids as the two of you were, but I told 'em ya'd be back!"

Karen simply got a hold of the black's mane and pulled herself up in front of Uzziah.

"I knew, too," she said, looking up at Uzziah with her big blue eyes.

My God, thought Uzziah, *she done lookin' like she's gonna be one beautiful woman when she growed up!"*

"Billy Patterson, how be ye?" Immanuel asked.

"Fine, now that yer here. These farmers were gettin' on my last boyhood nerve, not believin' that ya'd be back fer us!" he said, and he raised up his hand for Immanuel to shake.

Immanuel leaned down in the saddle and shook the boy's hand.

"We didn't come back fer ya," Immanuel said, and before he knew it, Billy left his feet, pulling the big man off his horse. Well, Immanuel let him do it. They both landed in a cloud of dust, then Billy was up in the big mountain man's face.

"Your promise ain't worth the nasty breath you used to give it, ain't that true!"

"Well, son—" Immanuel started to say, but halfway to getting up, he was pushed back down by Billy.

A crowd of soldiers was gathering and getting quite a kick out of this scene. Two mountain men were being roughed up by children!

"Yer a lying son of bitch!" Billy swore and pointed his finger into the face of Immanuel.

Immanuel could have taken a lot, but that boy pointing his finger not two inches from his nose, and now, there was a crowd gathering, and they were laughing, well, it was simply too much! He grabbed Billy and, turning him over his knee, he started swatting him on the rump.

Billy fought like a wildcat and kicked the mountain man a couple times in the head with his heels, but Immanuel just kept at it.

"That's enough, there, Immanuel. That there boy is like a son to me now!" It was Fred Trimble from the wagon train who, with his wife, had taken in the two Patterson children.

"Fred, it's good to see ya," Immanuel said, his hand in midair, about to strike Billy's rump again.

"Same here, Immanuel, but enough's enough!" Fred said as he took the boy's hand and helped him stand up. The boy was trying real fast to get up, then he ran off.

"Now, ya done it!" Fred quipped.

"Done what?" Immanuel asked.

"Ifn he gets it in his head to be obstinate, there ain't no changin' his mind. Yer punishments put him in his obstinate mood."

"Well, good for me, that's what I say!" Immanuel

said as he got to his feet and extended his hand to Mr. Trimble. They shook.

"Yer doin' a fine job of raising those kids, Fred." Uzziah felt it was time to ameliorate the situation between Immanuel and Fred before it got too out of hand,

"Thanks, Uzziah, you was always the level-headed one, weren't ya?"

"Now, just a minute, this big pup here is no better than a tenderfoot," Immanuel said.

"Do yer feet hurt?" Karen asked, looking up with her baleful eyes at Uzziah.

"No, sugar, my feet are fine, but thanks for caring," Uzziah said, petting her hair like she was a cocker spaniel.

"Well, is he right?" Fred Trimble asked, and by this time, several of the other settlers and farmers from that ill-fated wagon train had gathered around.

"Who was right and about what?"

"Billy, about you comin' to take us to Oregon!" one of the older men in the group who had gathered yelled.

"No, I mean, hell no! We is here to git whiskey and nothin' more!" Immanuel said.

The group that had gathered gave a collected sigh, and dispersed as if the wind had been let out of them.

Fred Trimble looked between Immanuel and Uzziah, "Might have known," he said, then spit on the ground between the two men.

"I think we just got insulted," Immanuel said, bowing up a bit.

"Well, here we are, makin' a good impression and all," Uzziah said, grinning.

"I'm gonna go see 'bout Billy," Karen said and

slipped off Uzziah's black horse as fast as she'd gotten up there.

———

The commissary had good bonded whiskey, and after supper, which Uzziah and Immanuel cooked in the open, not wanting to be beholding to the mess sergeant or anybody else, Immanuel opened one of the bottles and got about a third into it before Fred Trimble walked up.

"Fred," Uzziah said, not knowing what to expect.

"Uzziah," Fred said as he squatted down beside the fire the men had built to cook supper and stay warm.

"What do you want?" Immanuel asked.

"That ain't neighborly," Uzziah grunted.

"Last time I looked around our cabins in the mountains, we didn't have no neighbors," Immanuel spit out.

"The boy is truly hurt," Fred said.

"His butt?"

"No, fool, his pride," Fred spat back at him.

"Who you callin' a fool, old man?"

"Stop this right now!" Uzziah said, then added, "Where is the boy now?"

"In my wagon. Won't come out, neither for supper nor water. I'm worried about him."

"He'll get over it," Immanuel said, taking another sip from the bottle.

Uzziah got up, brushed off his deerskin pants, looked at Immanuel, and shook his head.

"Show me," was all he said, then he and Fred walked away.

Immanuel liked kids, he really did, but he knew

from the Bible that if you spared the rod, you spoiled the child. Not that he cared if the boy was spoiled, but he wouldn't have no youngster pointing a finger at his nose when he'd basically allowed himself to be taken off his horse. Although, he had to admit, that was a pretty good trick. He hadn't expected the boy to do that, and there weren't many things that Immanuel didn't expect, or at least figure might happen.

"Damn kid," he said under his whiskey breath.

———

Uzziah followed Fred Trimble to his wagon, and sure enough, the boy was lying down in there, and he had his eyes closed.

"He ain't asleep, ifn that's what ya was thinkin'," Fred said and walked back to his fire where his wife, a woman in her sixties with beautiful long white hair, was pouring him a cup of coffee.

"Billy," Uzziah said really soft like he was talking to a wild horse, "It's me, Uzziah. Immanuel wanted to come, but he's older than me and he's done fell asleep, son."

The boy sat bolt upright and stared at Uzziah.

"Don't make me hate both of ya," he said with grit in his voice.

"What ya mean?"

"Yer lyin', as simple as that, he ain't sleepin', he's gettin' drunk."

Uzziah was impressed that the boy knew that when men sought out whiskey, it wasn't long before they partook of it.

"Yer right, he's gettin' slouched."

"Why ya here?"

"I know why he's here," Karen said as she pulled on one of Uzziah's pant legs. He picked her up so she could see into the back of the wagon.

"Why? Ifn yer so smart, tell me," Billy demanded.

"He's here to apologize for his friend and to offer to take us all the way to Oregon, ain't ya, O?"

Uzziah looked at the little girl. She had called him the same nickname that he couldn't say her name now that she was dead, but it was the same name she called him. How'd she even know? How'd she even guess?

"What'd ya call me?"

"O," Karen said and looked directly into the big man's eyes.

"Why'd ya call me that?"

"I heard pa—"

"That old man ain't our pa!" Billy shouted loud enough for Fred to hear.

"I heard Mr. Trimble call you by your whole name, Uzziah Ferguson O'Something, and the onliest part I can remember is the O," she said.

"I see. Well, a very good friend of mine used to call me that, and I liked it," Uzziah said in a kind voice.

"Okay, O, then that's what I'll call ya," Karen said, hugging his neck.

"Mr. O'Bannon," Billy said, mostly showing his sister that he could remember the mountain man's name, "before ya left fer the mountains, me and Karen wanted to go with ya, remember?"

"Sure, I remember."

"And we couldn't 'cause Immanuel said there was no mountain women or girls."

"Yeah."

"But when I ask ya to promise me ya take us to Oregon, ya did, ya 'member that?"

"I do."

"And a promise is a promise, right?"

———

Uzziah left the kids there after he'd tucked them both into their beds in the wagon and told them a story. He told them how he and Immanuel had met the boy chief, Geronimo, and what a great warrior the boy was, and how they'd escaped, then gone back. Before he got Geronimo back to the Apaches, both the kids had fallen asleep. He climbed back down out of the wagon, and Fred and his wife were standing there.

"This is my wife, Gertrude," he said to Uzziah. "This here's Uzziah, a kind and gentle giant," Fred said and smiled.

"I got some apple pie I just made. Can I interest ya in a piece?"

Well, Uzziah hadn't had apple pie since his mama had made it for him, and naturally, he took the old woman up on it. As they walked the short distance to the fire, Gertrude took Uzziah's arm the way his ma did when they were walking together. Tears came to his eyes, and Gertrude saw them as he wiped them away.

"You okay, son?" Something his mother would have said, and the tears came again.

He had his pie, and it was, well, it wasn't his mama's pie, but it was sure good.

"Mind ifn I smoke?" he asked Gertrude.

"No, son, you go right ahead. Fred, join him," she said.

"Ya sure, ma?"

"I don't like the smoke in my face, but there's a nice little breeze, and I'm sitting upwind of both of ya," she said.

Uzziah tapped out his pipe and was offered tobacco from Fred's pouch, a gift that westerners gave when they liked somebody. They packed their pipes, and Uzziah took a burning twig from the fire and lit both their pipes.

"We have been waiting all spring for another wagon train, but there hasn't been any," Gertrude said. "I fear we'll be stuck here again. The fort's prices are eating into our homestead monies, and we got to have seed money when we get to Oregon. Have ya ever been?" she asked Uzziah.

"No, ma'am, I ain't, but I heard it's mighty purty."

"Where are ya headed after this?" Fred asked.

"Rendezvous up at Daniel City, Wyoming."

"Ain't that west of here?"

"About four hundred miles, I reckon."

"Hell, son, that's halfway to Oregon from here," Fred pointed out.

"Is it?"

"Can't ya at least take us that far? Maybe in Daniel City, we can find someone else to take us to Oregon, or maybe another wagon train will join up with us, and you can get shed of us," she said, and her voice, though normal, was sort of pleading.

"Ya got any more pie?" Uzziah asked.

2

Immanuel was having another dream. He was being rocked ever so gently by the angels. He was lying in a hammock under a weeping willow tree, and the sun was cutting through from time to time, and he had to squint when it did. He could hear the angels talking, but he couldn't make out what they were saying. It was probably best since men aren't supposed to talk to angels, or at least, he didn't think they were.

Finally, the branches parted mightily and the sun was burning a hole in his eyelid, even though it was closed. He opened his eyes, and across from him, sitting there looking at him sleep it off, were Karen and Billy.

"He's awake!" Billy screamed, and Immanuel's head felt like it was going to explode.

Immanuel again felt the motion of the wagon and tried to sit up but had to put both his hands to the side of his aching head. Boy, he felt like someone had hit him with a five-pound hammer.

"How's it goin', partner?" Uzziah asked as he rode

up behind the wagon on the swift black, who snorted as if he, too, were talking to Immanuel.

"What's goin' on? Why are we movin'?"

"Well, I realized something last night. We're goin' the same way the wagons are goin', and Daniel City is on the way to Oregon."

Immanuel fought his way to the end of the wagon and looked out. Fort Laramie was nowhere to be seen.

"Where's the fort?"

"About three hours thataway." Uzziah pointed behind the wagons that were following.

"You didn't!"

"Didn't what?"

"You did, didn't ya?"

"Make some sense," Uzziah suggested.

"You took advantage of my inebriated state and put me in Fred's wagon, didn't ya?"

"Are you feelin' better, Mr. Jones?" It was Gertrude who had turned on the buckboard and was talking back into the wagon.

"Who are you?"

"I'm Fred's wife, Gertrude. Glad to make your acquaintance," she said in a very nice voice.

"Same here," Immanuel said, then turned back to Uzziah, who had ridden off. "Son of a"—he looked and saw the children looking at him—"biscuit," he finished up. He tried climbing from the back of the moving wagon but got his heel caught on the tailgate and tumbled out of the wagon and into the road. No sooner had he hit the road than he got to his feet and looked around. Then, he saw his horse tied to the back of the Patterson's wagon. He walked up to it, and trying to mount up while the horse was moving was proving too much for him. He untied the horse and mounted up.

He kicked his horse up and moved to the front of the nine or so wagons. He wanted to count them, but his head hurt too much.

"What the hell have you done?" he shouted at Uzziah.

"Like I said, we're goin' to Rendezvous, just like ya wanted to, but we're traveling with these folks till we get to Daniel City."

"It will take us a lot longer to get there at this pace, old son!" Immanuel was angry. He knew he'd had too much to drink, and he knew he'd slept it off, but his partner of one year had no right to throw him in the back of some settler's wagon like he was a fifty-pound sack of flour.

"We'll still get there." Uzziah tried to make peace.

"Yeah, when everything that's interesting has already happened, and we'll get to hear all the good stories but not be a part of them," he said, then looked around and turned back to Uzziah. "You're right, we's goin' the same way, I tell you what. I'll see ya when ya get there," Immanuel said, and kicking up his horse, headed up the trail a lot faster than the wagons.

Uzziah almost took off after him, but what was he going to do, lasso him and make him ride with the settlers, as he called them. Then, it occurred to him that he could catch up and simply ride with Immanuel and forget about the wagons, but could he? No, he'd agreed for both of them to master these wagons as far as Daniel City. He'd told Fred and Gertrude that there would probably be somebody there who could take them the rest of the way. In either case, Immanuel was a spot on the horizon and would soon disappear. Uzziah wondered if this was the end of their partnership. Would he join back up with Uzziah when he showed up in Daniel City? Would he snub him and then, Uzziah wouldn't have a mountain man partner, nor any cabins in the Rockies?

———

Two days out of Fort Laramie, and still there was no Immanuel. *Boy, he really must have been pissed*, Uzziah thought. He ate each night with the Pattersons, and there was a good reason for that. He'd checked out the other wagons, and the women, or men, who cooked over their campfires were making things which, one, Uzziah didn't recognize, or two, Uzziah could smell what they were cooking, and it smelled just plain bad. He'd lucked onto the best cook in the wagon train and he was thanking his lucky stars. Still, when he went to bed down for the night by the fire, he missed Immanuel. They had been bunking close to each other for over a year, and not having him there was strange, strange indeed!

———

It was the third day after the wagon train left when an agent of the newly formed Pinkertons Agency rode into Fort Laramie. The Pinkertons were created by Allan Pinkerton out of Chicago, and their motto was *if no one else can catch them, we can*, or something like that. He rode up and tethered his horse, a nice-looking paint, to the railing outside the commander's headquarters. He was dressed in a black, close-fitting suit with long coat-tails and a hat that might have been a cross between a bowler and a fedora. It looked strange, but that was the hat he wore.

Inside the commander's office, he sat in his chair and enjoyed some coffee that had been offered to him. Well, he really didn't enjoy it because, as far as he could tell, it was made that morning, way before dawn.

"What's yer name again?" the captain asked, lighting a stinking cigar.

"Robert Spells," he said, wondering why the captain had forgotten his name in less than a minute.

"Well, Mr. Spells of the"—he stopped and looked down at the card that Robert had handed him on which, coincidentally, there was Robert's name on the embossed card—"Pinkerton Agency, how can I be of help? By the way, are you the law in Chicago?"

"No, we're a private detective agency that people turn to when other means of lawful investigating seem to have failed them."

"So, still, how can I be of help to you?"

"I was hired by a woman whose husband, who, by the way, was an undersheriff in Saint Louis when he disappeared. The high sheriff looked for him but paid no attention to what the undersheriff's wife told him about her husband's disappearance."

"When did he go missin'?"

"Over a year ago."

"Cold trail is what I would say," the captain said as he puffed the stinking cigar and blew the smoke not toward the ceiling but directly across the desk. Robert Spells coughed and covered his mouth and nose with a very white handkerchief.

"That'd be a good bandana to surrender with," the captain noted, still puffing away like a locomotive.

"We don't surrender," Spells said and coughed some more. "We find our man."

"Honorable sentiments, but what do ya have to go on?"

"The man by who the wife saw her husband dragged unconscious off their porch late at night was big, and he wore deerskins and a coonskin cap. After asking around, there was only one man who would have answered to that description, and I believe he probably came through here before last winter."

"You got a name on him?"

"Immanuel James Jones," Robert Spells, Pinkerton Agent, said, and he could tell by the way the captain reacted that he knew the name.

"You know the man, don't you?"

"I seen him."

"When?"

"Three days afore."

Robert Spells was so gladdened by the news that he stood up and knocked the straight-back chair he was sitting in over.

The corporal in the outer office opened the door. "Ya okay, Cap?" he asked, looking at the chair turned over on the floor.

"Yeah, fine, thanks, Corporal," the captain said, and the corporal shut the door.

"Do you have any idea where he is this very moment?"

"Funny you should ask me that," the captain started in.

"Why is it odd?"

"Ya see, I saw him ride in. They made quite an entrance, but when the other one left, I didn't see Immanuel with him."

"Who's the other one?"

"Uzziah O'Bannon, they're mountain men from the Rockies," the captain added.

"And you say you saw this Uzziah leaving. Which way was he going?"

"He's mastering a set of nine or so wagons west out of here on the Oregon Trail."

"May I supply up here, Captain?"

"Of course, but ya hafta pay at the commissary just like everybody else, don't care if you're pursuing killers or not."

"What makes you think I'm pursuing killers, Captain?"

"A man disappears for over a year, he's either leaving his wife 'cause she's terrible or he's dead, wouldn't ya say?"

———

As Robert Spells, Pinkerton Agent, rode away from the fort that night, he agreed with the captain's sentiments. More than likely, the undersheriff was dead. He wondered if the other man, Uzziah O'Bannon, had anything to do with the man's disappearance, and he'd already seen, down by one of the wood stations on the Mighty Mo, evidence of a man's slaying. Thigh bones, called femurs, were there and ropes had been used, and other human bones were scattered for a good three miles around that wood station. Something probably horrible had happened near that wood station, and Mr. Spells promised Allan Pinkerton that he would pursue this case to the end of the west if necessary. The agency was new, and Robert Spells wanted to make a name for himself within it. Finding the undersheriff's killer would do the trick.

———

Uzziah kept worrying about Immanuel. He just couldn't help it. They had been partners for just over a year, and he thought he knew the big man's mind, but he guessed that carrying him passed out to a wagon and absconding with him when he was passed out had somehow gone beyond the big man's ethos.

He was riding ahead of the wagons—he'd have to make a concerted effort to do a count—when he saw a wonderful sight. Up ahead of them, sitting on a big rock with his horse grazing on the mesquite nearby, sat Immanuel. He had made a small fire and coffee and was sipping the black brew when Uzziah, kicking up the black, had ridden ahead.

"Want a cup?" Immanuel asked. He seemed fine, like there was nothing wrong between them, so Uzziah went along. He took his tin cup from his saddlebags and, using a glove, poured the scalding brew in and took a sip.

"Terrible," he said and smiled at Immanuel.

"Well, what did ya expect, I did make it," he said, and the two men laughed.

"WAGH!" Immanuel yelled.

"WAGH!" Uzziah shouted back. Immanuel got up and the two big men embraced.

"Don't ya ever do nothin' like that to me again, pilgrim, understand?" Immanuel whispered in his ear.

"Yeah, never again!" Uzziah whispered and they both broke from the hug with the slapping of backs.

About that time, Fred Trimble's lead wagon came up and he stopped, all the others stopped behind him, and Uzziah took a head count. There were nine wagons in all, good now he knew.

"What's goin' on, fellas?" Trimble asked.

"Immanuel was just scouting the trail ahead, we're good to go," Uzziah said, and the two mountain men mounted up and rode ahead of the train as he started back up in its halting manner.

"When we gets to Daniel City, I'm breaking off and attending the Rendezvous, ya got that?"

Uzziah could tell there was no way around this mess of Rendezvous.

"Yeah, how long ya gonna be gone fer?"

"I'll be back when ya see me riding back," Immanuel said cryptically.

Uzziah grunted and nodded his head. It was as good as saying I understand, just fewer words.

———

They traveled for the rest of the day, and when they circled the wagons that night, a young woman came to where Uzziah and Immanuel were making their dinner.

"Have ya already made yer mess?" she asked, both men thinking she must have been associated with the army at some point. No civilian usually called supper *mess*.

"Well, I got this cheer bacon goin', but other than

that, we ain't got a thought," Immanuel said, thinking she was a beauty and a half.

"Well, my husband and I would like it if ya'd join us. We brought along some chickens and he has a hankering for it fried, ifn ya like it thataway?"

"Where ya at?" Uzziah asked, and she pointed directly across from where they were sitting. A man in a slouch hat waved when they looked his way.

They walked over, introduced themselves, and the young man, whose name was Clements Shaw seemed a bit wary of the men, but then again, that was the general reaction to mountain men to those who had never known one.

"So, you fellas live in the Rockies, do ya?"

"That's right, got me some cabins up there in the heights, and we trap beaver for their pelts," Immanuel said. "Why?"

It was a simple enough question, but the man looked like he was going through some very considerable thinking before he answered.

"Don't know, just always wanted to live where the majority of people don't live."

"Ya think Oregon might be the place?" Uzziah asked both of them since he looked between the woman who was turning the fresh fried chicken in grease and the man who was watching her.

"Yeah, we hope so," she answered too quickly.

The man had a scar on his right arm. It wasn't new, but it wasn't that old, either.

"Looks like ya seen some Injun action," Immanuel said, looking at the scar.

"Oh that, that's nothin'," he said as he pulled his sleeve down to cover it.

The dinner was excellent. They had brought some canned beans along, and there was the bacon that Immanuel had cooked. She'd even put a peach cobbler in a Dutch oven, and they had dessert.

"Ma'am, I got to tell ya, I ain't had peach cobbler like this since I left Virginia," Uzziah said.

"We never been to Virginia," the man named Clements Shaw lied in his Virginia accent.

"That so, then where ya from?" Uzziah asked.

"North Carolina," the woman lied.

They sat around and swapped stories, and the stories that the couple were most interested in were those about the mountains. There was something in the way their eyes got when they talked about being away from everybody and fending for themselves that caught Immanuel and Uzziah's attention.

Finally, they said their goodnights and went back to roll up in their bedrolls.

They were lying fairly close together, and Uzziah whispered to his partner.

"That man is from Virginia or I'm kin to a monkey."

"They was both lying like rugs. Couldn't tell when they spoke the truth to tell ya certain," Immanuel whispered back.

"What do ya think that was all about?" Uzziah asked.

"Ya see that wound, that scar on his right arm. My bet is that was made by some Injun."

"And so?"

"Hey, many a man has joined the US Army and then found that he didn't have the stomach to do what they wanted him to do. I figure he might be a prime case. They's talking about going into the wilderness. I'll bet ifn I asked them to come back with us to the cabins, they be all over that."

"Why?" Uzziah asked.

"My money says he's a deserter."

3

They left that morning and were within the five-mile range before noon. They circled the wagons and Uzziah said his goodbyes and made his requests as to what he wanted from the settlers. The two men parted company on a good note, and it was agreed that if trouble happened, Uzziah was to fire the Hawken twice as rapidly as he could to get Immanuel's attention.

The fourth day they were at their camp, Robert Spells, of the Pinkerton Agency rode into camp. There were men with rifles aimed at him as he came riding in, and before he had a chance to say a word, they had several rifles and a couple of shotguns on him. They recognized him as a tenderfoot, even more so than them because of the city suit and the strange hat he was wearing.

"Who are you and what are you doin' here?" Uzziah asked.

Spells was thrilled, he seemed to have found perhaps the very man he was looking for.

"Are you Immanuel James Jones?"

"That ain't the way this is gonna go," Uzziah said, lowering the Hawken that had become like a third arm to him on the stranger and cocking the piece.

"Now, hold on, stranger, I am Robert Spells with the Pinkerton Agency," he said this as if they would know what he was talking about.

"What the hell's a Pinkerton?" Uzziah asked, still pointing the Hawken at Robert.

"It's an investigative arm of armed men who go after ner-do-wells and other malcontents," Robert Spells said.

Off to the side, Uzziah noticed that Clement Shaw was quietly saddling one of his horses. *So*, thought Uzziah, *Immanuel was right, the man is wanted by the law. Well, come to think of it, they might be, since it was Immanuel that the man first asked for.*

Before Uzziah could say another word, Clement Shaw had taken his horse around to the backside of the wagon, and they could all hear a horse beating leather out of there.

Spells spurred his horse without saying another word and took off after Clement Shaw.

All the guns that had been trained on him lowered, and the company breathed a sigh of relief, all except Sally Anne, who ran over to Uzziah.

"You've got to help Clement, he's not that good a rider," she said to Uzziah.

"What's he wanted fer?" Uzziah asked.

She hung her head. "He deserted from the Second Dragoons down in Florida where they were fightin' the Seminoles," she said almost under her breath.

It was a habit that Immanuel had taught Uzziah: never unsaddle your horse until the day is done, then you may also want to keep it saddled if there's trouble nearby.

Uzziah hopped on the black and was out of the camp before anyone could ask him questions.

He turned in the saddle to see Trimble and some of the other men questioning Sally Anne, she would have to handle that on her own. Truth was, he couldn't see any private detective agency going after deserters. His thoughts immediately returned to what they had done in Saint Louis to that undersheriff, Randall Hicken. After all, hadn't they had a funeral for the woman whose name he could say no longer, and hadn't they paraded basically through the better neighborhoods of St. Louis on the way to the cemetery. Hadn't they threatened the local clergy if they wouldn't let them bury the poor whore. His eyes stung once again with the memory of her awful death, and then what they had done to the undersheriff. They were sure no one had seen them, but what if Randall's wife was up when Immanuel snuck up on his porch and knocked the man out and dragged him into the bushes?

After about ten minutes, he could see Clement Shaw up ahead of him in the foothills. He wasn't sparing the horse he was on, that was for sure. Then, coming from a swale, the Pinkerton Agent rode up and was very close behind the deserter. Shots were exchanged between the two men, and Shaw went sprawling off his horse and rolled down to a small stream. Spells rode down on him, covering him with his revolver as he did so.

Uzziah could see that neither man knew that he was following them. Neither had been concerned about anything else than being the hunted and the hunter.

Uzziah pulled the black off on a knoll, and getting off, he crawled on his belly to the top. Taking the spyglass, he looked down upon them.

———

"What are ya wanted for, son?"

Shaw realized just like that, that he wasn't the reason the detective had ridden into the circle of wagons. He was almost speechless with anger at himself and the way he'd tipped his hand.

"I ain't wanted," he said with little to no conviction.

"Oh, you just rode away from the wagon train like you'd seen the devil for no reason?"

"It ain't agin the law to take a ride on yer own horse," Shaw said again with little conviction.

Uzziah could see the man Robert Spells putting the handcuffs on Clement Shaw. There was going to be one disappointed Sally Anne when they got back to the wagons. What was Uzziah going to do? He did want to take the Pinkerton off Immanuel's scent, but how?

The scene down in the swale by the river wasn't getting any friendlier. Spells was pistol-whipping Clement.

———

Clement was bleeding badly and looked like he was scared to death.

"Why did ya run?" Spells asked him.

"Can't a man go for a ride on his horse?" Clement lied.

"Ya struck out of there like you was a shuck on fire."

"I ain't done nothin'," Clement replied.

"You know who Immanuel James Jones is?"

Clement was scared, he thought about just giving Immanuel up, but the two mountain men had been so gracious to him and his wife. He was still thinking about it when Spells swung his pistol and hit him in the face again.

————

Like most of us, Uzziah had a habit of talking to himself when the chips were down.

"What the hell ya gonna do, Uzziah? Ya done kilt one lawman, yer gonna go fer two?"

As he was saying this, he was pulling his Hawken up and aiming down at the swale by the river,

"I'm just gonna wing the son of a bitch, just wing 'em," he said as he threw a handful of dust in the air to get the windage.

"Easy, easy, easy," he said as the Hawken exploded, then he said, "Shit, now Immanuel will think there's trouble at the wagons, no wait, two shots, that's why we made 'er two shots." Uzziah laughed.

————

Down by the stream, which was babbling nicely when the pistol wasn't striking the side of Clement Shaw's face, Spells was about to hit the boy again when something like a big bee whizzed by and opened up the side of Robert Spells's head. The line appeared as the sound of the Hawken boomed over the hills. Blood ran down his face, and Spells sank to the ground, thinking that he'd been killed.

——

Uzziah rode down to where the Shaw boy was bleeding from all the pistol-whipping.

"You okay, son?"

"Ya kilt him, didn't ya?"

Uzziah dismounted and felt for a pulse on the side of Spells's neck.

"Nah, he ain't dead, just knocked out. Good thing I won so many turkey shoots back home in Virginia, where I know you and your wife Sally Anne are from," Uzziah said, not freeing the boy yet from the handcuffs.

"You don't know shit," Shaw said.

"You're a deserter, yer wife told me when ya ran off. Good thing, too, since ifn I hadn't come this way, ya'd probably be beat to death. The man does not have an easy way 'bout him, does he?"

"Take these cuffs off," Shaw demanded.

"In time," Uzziah said, as he inspected the crease on Spells's head. "He'll be fine. I seen wounds like this, and fellas can get mighty confused when a bullet kisses their head right on."

Uzziah got the key to the cuffs out of Robert Spells's pocket after that, he bandaged Spells's head all the way around. Immanuel had taught him to carry bandages of some kind just in case.

"I think we should kill 'im," Clement Shaw said.

"Ya do, huh, well, here," Uzziah said, handing Clement his gun back. "You go right ahead and drill this man. Think ya feel guilty now, but just wait 'til ya take a human life."

Clement held his gun and cocked it right at Spell's body, center mass. His hand began to tremble, and he lowered the gun.

"Didn't think ya was a killer, most aren't," Uzziah said, then added, "Git yer horse and mount up, we's gonna go the rest of the way to the rendezvous and seek some advice."

———

They rode the other couple miles, and when they got to the top of a ridge, below them, there was a falderal of a mass of men doing just about anything you could imagine. Some men were throwing Injun hatchets at a target, some were poking squaws just barely off the trail, some trading pelts, some drinking whiskey, some just smoking pipes and watching the two strangers who rode in. They wouldn't have been worried about Uzziah, he'd spent enough time with Immanuel to look the part, but those other two—well, one was tossed across a saddle and looked half dead, and the other was obviously a farmer or something.

Uzziah didn't see Immanuel before he was seen by him.

"Wagh!" Immanuel shouted, and Uzziah turned his horse in that direction.

"Thanks for bringing dinner, but there's only a couple of us who actually eat humans," Immanuel said and laughed. Those around him chuckled and passed the jug which obviously Immanuel had had a portion of.

Uzziah and Clement dismounted and came over. Spells was still like a dead man hanging over his horse.

"What happened, partner?"

Uzziah sat on a log and explained everything that was going on. Immanuel was thinking about it when Spells woke up.

"What!? Where!? Get me off this horse!" Spells demanded.

They carried him to where the circle of men was and laid him down.

"Who are you men? What's the meaning of this!?" Spells was more agitated than mad, which gave Uzziah a thought.

"Who are you, mister?"

Spells looked around as if he were in a dream.

Spells hesitated, started to speak, then jumped up, swayed on his feet, and passed out.

"You men, strip him," Immanuel asked a couple of other mountain men, who laughed and were so drunk they were game for anything,

"We gonna cornhole 'im?" one of them asked.

"I am gonna forgit ya asked such a disgusting thing. What's the matter with ya? There's plenty of squaw quim around at low prices. Ya need satisfaction, seek it there," Immanuel berated the man who had, in reality, only made a joke.

"Was only kiddin'," the man said as he and the other fella stripped Spells 'til he was bare naked.

"Go gather some deerskins, moccasins, and a coon-skin cap, we gotta make some alterations here," Immanuel said.

"Are we doin' what I think we're doin'?" Uzziah asked.

"Some men with head wounds ain't good at 'memberin', we gonna help him fergit," was all Immanuel said.

The two returned with a hodgepodge of mountain man clothing and dressed the Pinkerton Agent. Immanuel took a straight razor and Shaw thought he was going to cut the man's throat when he took the razor over there, but all he did was shave his head as clean as a whistle. Immanuel rubbed some bog moss on his head and made it look dirty, like the man had always worn his hair like that. Once he was dressed, they sat him by the fire, put the jug between his legs, and waited.

The party continued as different mountain men came and went. They all thought it was a great joke, but one spoke up out of turn.

"What ifn the headshot didn't make him lose his memory?"

"Then, we'll have to kill 'im," Immanuel said, "I'm pretty sure me and Uzziah know why he's out this way."

Around midnight, Robert Spells woke up. The first thing he did was pick up the jug and take a swallow. After he swallowed, he jumped up and ran to the pond nearby and jumped in. Everybody was laughing when he came back.

"What in the name of Jesus H. Christ is in that jug, kerosene?"

"Just moonshine," Immanuel said, waiting to see if the man remembered who he was.

Robert Spells then rubbed his hands over his head and smiled. It was obvious he didn't have a clue what was going on.

"How long have I been here, wherever here is?"

"Two, three days," one man offered.

He picked up the jug and took another swig, this time, he didn't require the pond to ease the pain.

He reached up and touched the bandage around his head. "What happened to me?"

"You got in an argument with Immanuel here, and both of ya shot it out. Lucky fer you, Immanuel was drunker than you, grazed yer head, coulda kilt ya," Uzziah said, getting into it.

Shaw hadn't said a word, and he, also, had been given deerskin clothes and he looked the part. Robert Spells looked right at him.

"What you looking at?" Spells asked Shaw.

"Nothin'," Clement Shaw said, and Robert Spells went back to drinking.

———

Immanuel and Uzziah decided to send Clement Shaw back to the wagons and let them know everything was all right. Uzziah let Clement take his Hawken and told him about firing two shots in rapid succession if something was wrong.

The rendezvous was about over. Immanuel had missed a great deal of it, but now, they thought it their special pleasure to make sure Robert Spells got an education in what it meant to be a mountain man.

First, they took him over to the squaw that had been servicing all of them.

"This here is Rose Water," Immanuel said to Robert. "Rose Water, this here is Robert. He needs a poke."

"How much?" Robert asked, at least he was familiar enough with what came with a poke.

"You nice, I give special price. Fifty cents?"

That was high, but what did Robert know, maybe he was even a virgin, they didn't care.

When they looked back over there, it seemed he was paying for another ride, he mounted back up and had at it.

"How long will he not remember?" Uzziah asked, looking a bit worried.

"Knew a fella twenty years ago, got hit in the head by a tomahawk, never did know anything but what happened after he was hit. Died a different man than when he began. But truthfully, we all liked him better after he'd almost been kilt," Immanuel said, thinking back.

"I remember him, John something or other, right?" one of the other mountain men said.

"John Neverminded is what we used to call him," Immanuel said with a laugh.

"He didn't mind either, did he?" the same mountain man said and laughed along with Immanuel.

———

They spent the next two days partying. They weren't worried about the wagons since no one had been hostile anywhere near Daniel City, which was nothing more than a sundry store and an old man and his equally old squaw.

Immanuel had been right to get the bonded whiskey at the fort, the other stuff, which Robert Spells was doing his best to drink every day, gave a big headache the next day, unless ya continued drinking.

Uzziah and Immanuel gathered a bunch of old, wily mountain men around them.

"What's up, boss?" one of them asked.

"Someone's got to take Robert off our hands," Immanuel said, looking around.

Just about everyone was busy looking down at the ground except one really old timer.

"Well," he said, "he's strong, and I'll need help this winter, I'm sure."

Someone went and got Robert, who had run out of money and was begging Rose Water for another poke.

"She won't take credit," Robert said to the group.

"No, whores like their monies up front," Uzziah said, speaking from experience, then added, pointing to the older mountain man, "You remember Jedidiah Younger?"

Robert looked at the man up and down.

"No, is he somebody I know?"

"Son, we've been partnerin' up for the past five years. I done taught you everythin' ya know about these cheer mountains," the old man said, looking forlorn like he'd lost his best friend.

"Don't you worry, Jedidiah, I'll remember soon 'nough," Robert said. "Do we live near here, near enough for me to get a poke from Rose Water from time to time?"

"Nah, we's on the other side of the mountains, but here, partner, here's a dollar, go git yerself two pokes afore we leave," Jedidiah said, and Robert hugged the old man, who pushed him away. "Guessin' ya done forget I don't like to be hugged!"

"Sorry, but thanks," Robert said as he ran off, waving the dollar above his head.

4

When they got back to the wagons, everyone there was ready to move on. They were there early in the morning and not wanting to hang around just in case Robert Spell came around to realizing who he really was.

As Uzziah had passed out all the goods that different ones had asked him to get at the sundries store, and they were riding away, Uzziah turned to Immanuel.

"We didn't give him a name!"

"Who, Spells? Well, old Jedidiah was callin' him Toby last time I saw them together. Hey, ya probably changed that man's life for the good, old son."

"Just glad we didn't have to kill another lawman."

"Question is, is a private detective a lawman?"

"Don't rightly know."

"Me neither, but we done a good thing, sending another man into the mountains. Plus, he might still be a virgin ifn it hadn't been for Rose Water."

"Is that her real Injun name?" Uzziah asked.

"Old son, sometimes I think—I don't know what I

think—no, we call her that, well you got a poke from her, does she smell like rose water?"

"Nah, kinda smells like fish gone bad."

"So?"

"Oh, I guess that's kinda cruel. Ifn she knew."

"She knows, and believe me, she could give a shit. I saw her one year gut a man who tried to beat her when he was humpin' her. His guts spilled right out on top of her. She brushed them off, got up, and kicked the dying man in the head. Don't you worry about Rose."

They traveled the rest of the day without incident. Then, as the sun was getting ready to set, and there was to be only an hour or so of light left, Immanuel and Uzziah were looking for a safe place to camp, near water, but not exactly sticking out like a sore thumb. They found a cliff that ran along a river that they ran into, and they decided to camp down by the river. There was a nice sandy beach, and as they pulled down beside the river, a shot rang out!

Uzziah and Immanuel were looking around for Injuns or bad hombres when there came a scream from one of the wagons. They rode back to the wagon where all the screaming was going on. The man who had been driving it was lying across the buckboard seat and bleeding profusely.

"What happened? Who shot him?" Uzziah asked.

The woman, who was keening and bawling like a calf, kept pointing to the man's rifle, which was lying near the toe board.

Immanuel picked it up and smelled the barrel.

"Shot by his own rifle," he said as several men got him down from the buckboard and laid him in the sand.

"It ain't as bad as it looks," Fred Trimble said. He and Billy were tending to the man,

"I want all you people to not, repeat, *not* put a round in the chamber of your rifles or pistols, do ya understand me?" Immanuel shouted to all those standing around, and in the next few minutes, all you could hear was the ratcheting of rounds from rifles.

"Shall we camp here?" Uzziah asked.

"Well, that was the idea 'til someone shot themselves, don't see no reason why we shouldn't continue on with it," Immanuel said.

———

They made a semi-circle of wagons against the stream, which had a nice flow to it. The end of two wagons almost had their back wheels in the water. It seemed like everyone's mood had improved as soon as they found that the man had been wounded by a through and through. There was no slug to take out, and therefore, he wouldn't die of lead poisoning. They had no doctor with them. Although Immanuel had been known to treat gunshot wounds.

After they'd all eaten and settled in for the night, they watched a thunderstorm that was so far away you could barely hear the thunder. It made a light show that a person would have paid a pretty penny to see if it had been fireworks. Their conversations were backdropped by this continuous light show, and even when most of the fire had died to embers, the lightning continued.

Now, Immanuel was a mountain man, and Uzziah

was from Virginia. Neither one of them had been out this far west, and neither had the settlers, or pilgrims, as Immanuel called them. What they didn't know was that they had camped in an arroyo. It was a place where water ran when there was water, but when it was more or less dry, then only a spring ran through it. Many miles to their north, the water that had come down from the violent thunderstorms that they had enjoyed was gathering steam and crashing through the ravines where it naturally flowed.

Immanuel was still awake when he heard something like a freight train coming from the north. Thankfully, most of the pilgrims were sleeping in their wagons since the fear was the lightning storms would be coming their way.

Immanuel kicked Uzziah and grabbed as much of their stuff as he could.

"Get up! Get up!" he yelled and as he dragged Uzziah to where the cliffs had been carved out, and they could see their horses running in front of them, the water came down the arroyo.

It was five feet high, and it swept most of whatever it encountered before it. Branches, trash, old wagon wheels, rocks, they were all in the mix. The two wagons closest to the river got blasted and turned around. Uzziah could hear the poor people inside screaming but couldn't see much.

The sound of the freight train lasted for about five minutes and it was quiet once again, except for the moaning and crying of the pilgrims.

They went around as best they could in the dark and gathered people up by the cliffs. Immanuel soaked some rags in pitch and lit them. They made good torches. Seven of the wagons hadn't been bothered, but two had been churned up in the now big river and were nowhere in sight. The man who had been resting on the beach was gone!

————

They waited until sunrise, and Uzziah, Immanuel, and some of the men who had riding horses went downstream to see what they could see.

About two miles down, they found one wagon. It had been toppled over.

Uzziah tied a rope around himself and secured it to his saddle on the black and waded out into the river, which was swift. He stumbled once and the black had to back up to get Uzziah back on his feet again.

When he got to the wagon, which was snagged on a big tree that had been washed along with the flood and now had dug into the bottom of the river, Uzziah grabbed hold and, pulling himself along, got to the rear end of the wagon and looking inside, he saw a man with his arms around a young woman. They had drowned in each other's arms, and really, Uzziah thought, they looked peaceful.

He had two ropes tied around him, and now he untied the one as he climbed inside the nearly water-filled wagon.

"Sorry about this, y'all," he said. He was a bit embarrassed for the woman because the water had taken most of her dress off from the waist up. He looked at her bosom and blushed even though she was dead. He managed to pull the dress up around her and tied the rope around both bodies.

It was then that the snag loosened, and the wagon made a groaning sound like it was about to move, and it did. Uzziah knew that if he or the couple were caught inside the wreckage, his black wouldn't be able to keep from being pulled into the river and drowned.

He tried to take them in his arms and make his way toward the back of the wagon, but things scraped and moaned, and the wagon tumbled over, taking him and the couple downstream.

———

On the shore, the black tried to hold his own but was jerked off his legs and pulled into the river, but then, he was released.

"Uzziah cut the rope," Immanuel said as he rode like the wind after the tumbling wagon.

———

Inside the wagon, Uzziah let go of the drowned couple, and each time his head was above water, he took a deep breath and then went back under with the tumbling wagon. Supplies in the wagon were bouncing off the big man, and he covered his head with his arms to keep from getting knocked out.

———

On the shore, Immanuel was riding alongside the tumbling wreckage, calling out, "Uzziah! Uzziah, get the hell out of there!"

Finally, the wagon tongue got caught on something

on the bottom, and the whole shebang flipped arse over teakettle and floated on its back, twisting downstream, but now upside down.

Immanuel left his horse, dropped his weapons, ran as fast as he could, and dove off into the wild water. He hit the water above where the wagon was caught and, in no time at all, was grabbing hold and taking a deep breath. He swam under the wagon and into the box. The water was muddy, so he couldn't see a thing, but he grabbed a naked woman, and he thought for a moment his ex-wife had come back from hell to drown him. He struggled to the surface with the woman's body and a rope was thrown to him. He grabbed hold, and as his horse backed up, he and the naked woman were pulled from the raging torrent.

When he was dragged onto the shore, he looked up and Uzziah was sitting on his horse.

"How in the hell?" Immanuel asked.

"I's about to ask ya the same," Uzziah said.

Billy had ridden down behind Immanuel and he explained the whole thing.

"Ya was swimming toward the wagon when Uzziah comes out the one end, and ya took a deep breath and went in the opposite end," he excitedly said.

"There was a man, too, did ya see him?"

"See 'em, I think he and I went a coupla rounds before I grabbed his lady friend," Immanuel said, then he and Uzziah both realized that Billy was staring at the naked, drowned woman.

Immanuel pulled down his suspenders, took off his wet shirt, and covered the top of the woman. Her legs were still sticking out. About that time, three other riders showed up, including Mr. Trimble.

He dismounted and flipped the wet shirt back to see the woman's face. "She had a husband," Fred said, and Uzziah and Immanuel pointed downstream, "and a baby!"

"Did you see a baby afore all went to hell?" Immanuel asked Uzziah.

He shook his head no.

———

They returned with the woman's body draped over the horse that Billy had ridden down to the accident. Billy rode behind Immanuel.

"What are these marks on your back?" Billy asked.

"Ain't nothin'," Immanuel said.

Billy looked over to Uzziah, who had never seen his partner's back. Uzziah had seen such marks back in Virginia, but they had always been on runaway slaves. He shrugged his shoulders to Billy, who let it drop.

When they got back to where they'd camped, the woman whose husband had been accidentally shot was crying. His body was never found. One of the women had heard a baby crying on the other side of the cliffs and found the couple's baby. There was no explanation other than supernatural that would account for the baby's survival. Everyone agreed that an angel of the Lord had come down and taken the baby from the wagon. Then, they remembered the baby's name was Isaac, which in Hebrew meant child of laughter.

"Was they religious?" Uzziah asked the woman who seemed to know them best.

"No, not particularly," she said.

"Well," Immanuel said, "God spares whom he spares." And that was that.

The other wagons had been tossed around some, but nobody was hurt except Karen, who had a lump on the back of her head like a goose egg. She had a headache, and Immanuel fixed her some arnica. He ground the plant up and made a tea for her. She said she didn't like the taste, but it helped her head.

They buried the young woman, and Uzziah was asked to read the Bible over the grave.

"This here young lady died in the arms of her husband. I saw 'em before the wagon tumbled and it almost got me. They looked so happy in each other arms. I'm sorry we couldn't have brought them both back here to be buried together," he said, then he read Psalm 23, which everyone appreciated.

Another young couple who had had trouble having children decided they would take the baby.

5

Toby, a.k.a. Robert Spells, the Pinkerton Detective, was doing a fine job for Jedidiah. They had made it to the old man's digs, and they weren't bad. He had a cabin front built around a cave opening, and they slept in the back of the cave, and cooked and had a stove in the front part, which simply looked like a cabin cut in half.

The old man was sitting, watching Toby cut wood, and he hadn't seen anybody do that with such aplomb since, well, he couldn't remember when.

Toby wasn't thinking about anything. He was into the flow of the wood cutting just the way he did...he almost had a memory. He used to cut wood like this for someone else—a mother, perhaps? He stopped and, leaning on the axe handle, let the sweat run down his back, and it almost came again, those of whom he used to cut wood for, but then, as soon as it had almost appeared, it disappeared again. Maddening, that's what it was.

"Hey, Mr. Jedidiah, how long ya say we been humping these mountains together?"

"Well, you came up here a couple years ago, thought maybe ya was in trouble of some kind." The old man loved lying. Lying was one of his favorite sports, right next to tall tales. Sometimes, he got the tall tales mixed up with the lying, and he was about to make that mistake right now, but he checked himself. Was about to tell Toby he'd ridden in on a tall frog. He'd save that one for one of the kids at the trading post.

"What kinda trouble?" Toby asked.

"I never found out, ya was so closed-mouthed about it. Heck, now it looks like I'll never find out how bad an hombre ya are."

Toby went back to chopping wood, and Jedidiah relit his pipe and with a smile of satisfaction, he blew the smoke into the Ponderosa pines that surround his cabin/cave.

The old man knew he'd have to show Toby how to set traps, clean pelts, and the whole shooting match, but he didn't mind. Telling someone—someone who was going to help you—how to do things was a pure joy, compared to actually doing them yourself.

They spent the next few months cleaning traps, fixing up the front cabin, cleaning out the stovepipe, and just getting everything ready for the winter. Jedidiah had explained about the traps and shown the boy how to do things without actually getting in the water. When the fall season came, he would take him out and let him get his feet wet, literally.

Every once in a while, while Toby worked, he'd stop and it looked to Jedidiah that he was remembering some

things, but every time he asked him what he was thinking, he'd just say *nothing*.

———

The wagon train of now seven wagons had made it as
far as the Idaho territories. The rightful owners of that
part of the country were still under dispute. The British
still thought of it as theirs, and so did the French. The
British called it the Columbia District, and it was
patrolled every once in a while by British troops who
were, in essence, simply working for the Hudson Bay
Company, and their job was to keep trappers from
taking furs from the Columbia District.

And so, it was as the little wagon train rolled down
into a fertile valley with mountains on both sides that a
troop of some fifteen British soldiers, their uniforms not
exactly squared away, and the hats they wore as various
as a parade of hats at Easter in a big Eastern Church
service, came riding down out of the hills.

Uzziah had the spyglass out and was glassing them.

"Who the hell are these guys?" Immanuel asked.

"Oh good," Mr. Trimble said, he'd been riding with
them up front. "It looks like we might have a military
escort the rest of the way."

Both Immanuel and Uzziah looked at each other.
Their expressions told the varied story of what these
fifteen men could mean. They were obviously British,
but their lack of military discipline suggested that they
might be a rogue band simply using the uniforms to
trick people into trusting them.

The captain of the group, a man in his early thirties
and wearing his uniform totally buttoned up and

squared away but wearing the head of a grizzly bear as a hat, held up his hand and stopped the other fourteen who were riding two by two behind their captain, They all were more or less dressed properly, but many tunics were unbuttoned, and all their hats were, it seemed, a contest as to who could be the most outrageous. One man even had on a bonnet with it tied under his chin.

"Good day," the captain said and the bear's head moved with his talking, "I am Captain Reginald Thomson."

"Good day, Captain," Immanuel said, then added, "How may we be of assistance to His Majesty's Mounted dragoons?"

The captain looked at Immanuel as if to question his knowledge of the British Cavalry, but he let it drop.

"Oh no, sir, we are here to be of assistance to you people," the captain said in his fine British accent.

Immanuel looked at Uzziah, then spoke, "Well, as you can see, we seem to have these few wagons well under our control." As he was speaking, several men broke ranks and rode along the five wagons. Comments could be heard by these men referring to some of the young women with them.

"Really, Captain, is it your practice to let your men make rude comments to young ladies?" Uzziah asked, and you could see the captain getting angry, but both Hawkens were loaded and more or less pointed at the man.

"Bentley, Rogers, get back here," the captain ordered them, but as they rode back, they both sneered at the two mountain men.

"So, we'll be on our way," Immanuel said, hoping it would be the end of the matter.

"I think not," the captain said, then added, "There's been reports of new Injun activity, and we wouldn't feel right leaving such a vulnerable target for the red man to take advantage of. We will ride with you to the Dalles."

"Well, we ain't seen hide nor hair of no Injuns fer many a moon, what makes ya think we'll have trouble?" Immanuel wanted to know.

"Oh, you will, you will," the captain said, then he ordered his fourteen men to ride seven on each side of the wagons. Many of the people welcomed them, thinking they were safer now with a military escort, even a military escort with funny hats.

Uzziah and Immanuel, along with Mr. Trimble, were still up front as the captain saw fit to ride along the wagons and introduce himself to any woman on the train.

"Ain't he a smug son of a bitch!" Trimble said as he was watching the captain flirt with his wife. Then Billy got on the captain's horse with him and seemed thrilled.

"I don't like that, I don't like that one bit," Uzziah said.

"They're up to something," Immanuel said. "Did ya notice those two who rode back there on their own? They had scalps hanging from their reins."

"So do you," Uzziah reminded Immanuel.

"I know, but I'm a good guy, who are they?"

The rest of the day went by without incident, but by supper, when they had circled there in the long valley, and the food was prepared, and the whiskey was brought out by the Brits, things got a bit tense.

Toby was resting in front of the cabin, the half-cabin that was built in front of the entrance to the cave. Jedidiah had gone hunting, and Toby was taking the opportunity to rest. The old man had worked him like a slave ever since they got there. He understood, he was the younger and the stronger of the two of them, but deference has its limitations. While he had his feet up and he was ruminating about his present situation, he fell asleep and had a dream.

———

In the dream, he was not a mountain man, but a man of the law. He looked down and could see that he had some kind of star on his chest. He wanted to take the badge off and read what it said, but he was standing over a man who was bleeding badly from his face. He looked at his pistol, and there was blood on it. His stomach turned as he realized he must have been hitting the man in the face with the gun.

"What have you done wrong?" he asked the man, wanting to know if this behavior he was manifesting warranted this pistol-whipping.

"I told ya, I ain't done nothing wrong," the man said with a slight Virginia accent, and immediately, Toby knew who that man was. He had run when he'd challenged a group of people about the real man he was searching for. But for the life of him, he could not remember the name of the man he was really looking for.

"Who am I looking for?" he asked the bloodied Virginian.

"How the hell should I know? Ya run me down on

my horse and start beatin' me with no explanation whatsoever!" The man was obviously upset.

"Who am I after?"

"Well, it ain't me, Mr. Pinkerton!" the Virginian said, and Toby woke up from the dream.

———

He was so startled that he stood immediately and almost lost his balance and fell, but he righted himself by grabbing the edge of the cabin. About that time, Jedidiah rode up with a deer across the back of the horse he was riding.

"Got us a good un!" he yelled as he rode in, letting the deer fall from the back of the horse, in front of Toby.

"You gut 'im and clean him up, we'll have venison steaks tonight."

"No!" was all Toby said.

Jedidiah circled his horse once and looked down upon Toby, who might just know he wasn't Toby anymore.

"What ya mean, no?"

"Who am I?"

"What the hell kinda fool question is that?" Jedidiah asked, thinking that for sure, he was about to lose his helper.

Toby reached up and jerked the old man off his horse, pulled his pistol, cocked it, and set it against Jedidiah's head.

"Talk or die!"

"You ain't Toby."

"Tell me something I don't know."

"You rode into Rendezvous already shot up. That

wound on yer head was caused by a Hawken. Yer lucky yer alive, son."

"And my real identity?"

"Don't know, there was these two fellas, I knew one of 'em, name of Immanuel, and he was all set on trickin' ya into believin' ya was somebody else."

"Toby?"

"I gave ya that name."

"What's my real name? Tell me, or so help me God, I'll plaster the ground with your brains."

"Here," Jedidiah said and tossed a wallet and badge down at Toby's feet.

Toby, or as he was about to find out, Roger Spells, forgot all about the old mountain man he'd dragged off his horse and threatened to kill. He holstered the pistol and picked up the badge and wallet. He had opened the wallet and was inspecting the badge when Jedidiah clubbed him with the butt of his Hawken. He went down like a felled tree.

"Ya been a lot of help, but no man sticks a pistol in my face in my own house," Jedidiah said as he reached down and picked up the badge and wallet.

————

That night, as Immanuel and Uzziah were about to turn in, they were hunched around their small fire and talking.

"They sure are taking all the attention and the food," Uzziah complained as Sally Anne had killed another chicken and fried it up for the captain and his corporal. The others had taken up with the other wagons, the other settlers.

"All this being friendly and thankful for a military escort may be just the preamble to some real bad business," Immanuel said.

"You don't believe them for a moment, do ya?"

"Look, I know, I mean, I heard at Rendezvous that the Pacific Fur Company has folded, and everything they had and the trading post and all has been turned over to the Hudson Bay Company. The French are getting pushed out, and that's fine by me, but these hombres, their hats, man, what is goin' on with that?"

"My favorite is the guy with the bonnet," Uzziah remarked.

"Yeah, well, ifn ya saw his reins, he'd got blond hair dangling from them, and that blond hair woulda looked real good with that bonnet surrounding it."

"Ya think..." Uzziah started and stopped.

"They is rebels sure 'nough. They will cut all our throats and ransack every wagon here. The women, and even the girls, thinking about Karen now, they'll all be raped then murdered," Immanuel whispered in his angry rasping whisper.

"Tonight?"

"No, tonight is a scouting mission. They're checking out who has what weapons, who has women folk, whose throats to cut first, and so on."

"I guess that puts us at the top of the list," Uzziah offered.

———

Roger Spells woke up, remembering who he was and also remembering it probably wasn't a good idea to turn his back on Jedidiah. He was tied to a tree, and it was dark and getting colder. Then, as he was struggling with the ropes, it began to rain. *Great*, he thought, *now I'm going to be miserable, wet, and tied up!*

"Hey, old man, this ain't exactly a spring rain!"

Jedidiah came to the door of the cabin. He had a steaming bowl of venison stew in his hand, and with a wooden spoon, he was helping himself to large portions and chewing as only someone who has lost a lot of teeth chews.

"That looks good," Robert said, trying to be nice.

"Shoulda thought of that afore ya pulled me off my horse, son. That was rude."

"I am sorry—"

"No man has ever done that to me, and no, ya ain't, and now ya know yer some highfalutin lawman or something. I seen yer kind afore, and there's nothin' yer ever sorry fer," he said as he started to close the door to the cabin, "Gettin' a bit nippy out here with the rain and all."

"Don't leave me out here!"

———

When the false dawn was on the camp, Uzziah and Immanuel were up early. Uzziah knew exactly where Billy and Karen slept. He whispered down to the Trimble's wagon, and sneaking up on Fred sleeping on the ground, he put his hand over his mouth.

"It's just me," he said, and Fred relaxed.

"What are ya doin'?"

"We're takin' Karen and Billy and goin' fer help," Uzziah whispered.

"Why?"

"Immanuel got a gut-feelin', and he's generally right."

Fred just nodded his head and stayed in his bedroll as Uzziah got both kids up and carried them almost asleep, one in each arm, as he went back to where Immanuel had the horses.

Then, with neither of the kids really knowing what was going on, they snuck out of the camp. They had a plan, well, Immanuel had a plan, and it wasn't exactly to Uzziah's liking, but he'd be damned if he could come up with anything better.

They rode quietly away from the camp and headed north by northwest. He heard some of the *soldiers* talking about the Paiutes who live north of here.

"So," Uzziah began, "ya think these Injuns, these Pie-utes will help us with these soldiers?"

"Son, those Brits are a bunch of yellow-bellied no-counts who prey on women and old men. We get some Injuns of any kind down upon them, and they will scatter like nobody's business."

"But what ifn the Pie-utes think we're the enemy?" Billy asked, pronouncing the tribe's name the way Uzziah did.

"We'll cross that nasty bridge when and ifn we get to it," Immanuel said as he continued leading the way north.

"What if when the soldiers realize we're gone they just kilt everybody?" Karen asked, worried about Fred and his wife.

"If we find the Injuns, this will happen way afore they get a chance to do mischief," Immanuel insisted.

———

Robert Spells was shaking uncontrollably when Jedidiah emerged from the cabin. He looked up at the old man like he wanted to kill him.

"Don't be givin' me no death stares, ya varmint. I treated ya like a partner, and tossing me off my horse was my reward?"

"Old man, when I git outta these ropes, I will string ya up with 'em, ya hear me?"

"Thought about that. I'm gonna go see a friend. Be gone fer a few days."

"And yer gonna leave me all alone?"

"Nah," the old man said as he brought from the cabin a small coffee can. He pulled his knife from its scabbard and Roger Spells started screaming at the top of his lungs, "Ain't nobody close enough to hear ya, but there's plenty close enough to smell ya," he said as he dipped the big-bladed knife into the bacon grease in the can, and smeared it all over Robert Spells. "Yer gonna be one tasty treat," Jedidiah said, tossing the rest of the bacon grease into Roger's face, momentarily blinding him with the cold grease.

————

The village was up ahead. Immanuel had seen the thin lines of smoke trailing up to the early morning sunrise. There were a bunch of wikiups gathered around a central firepit. As they rode in, braves came out and made threatening gestures, but Immanuel used sign language to tell them that they meant no harm. Having the children with them helped. Billy got down and started playing with some kid who was chasing a hoop.

They were finally shown to the wikiup of someone

in charge, maybe a chief. Immanuel used his signing skills once again, and the man who wasn't that old and may have been the chief laughed out loud.

"What did you tell him?" Uzziah asked.

"I asked him to attack the wagon train with us."

"What?!"

"Look, I made it clear we weren't really going to hurt anybody in the wagons, we just want to see the Brits run. It seems they know about these so-called soldiers and they've caused some trouble for them before."

Immanuel made it clear that time was of the essence, but it seemed no Injuns wanted to do anything without the pipe smoke coming first.

———

When they left the camp, there must have been fifty-sixty braves with them. Some had rifles, some bows and arrows, some just rode along to make a lot of dust and holler.

When they came down on the wagon train, they had already pulled up stakes and were traveling west. The wagons were about to leave the long valley, and the place where the valley ended was narrow, with steep walls on each side.

Immanuel had Paiutes climb up into the hills where the cliffs were, and the rest he had come up around behind the wagons.

When the Paiutes screamed from the top of the cliffs and the others rode hard from behind, screaming at the top of their lungs. Immanuel had been right. Realizing that the wagons couldn't be pulled into a circle, the British dragoons saw only one direction that there were no Injuns, and they took off that way.

Immanuel was down by the wagons by the time the Paiutes showed up. The settlers were relieved. The soldiers that night had made demands on some of the young women, and even though they refused, the dragoons had made it clear that if they wanted safe passage, the young women better start cooperating.

The Paiutes had been promised material, coffee, powder, and shot for their troubles. The older ladies in the wagon train got out the bolts of cloth they had with them, and the Paiutes only took a bit from each bolt.

Immanuel was signing with the chief and they agreed to help the wagons get all the way to the Dalles. The Dalles were a series of rapids that wound their way down the Columbia River toward the ocean. At certain times of the year, these rapids were possible to be traversed, but at other times, they were deadly.

———

The first critters to show up where Robert Spells was tied up were small. Badgers, raccoons, squirrels, and deer. He was surprised so many of them wanted to lick the grease. But there they were, coming up to him cautiously and sometimes in numbers. The raccoons finally came right up to him, even as he was screaming at them to get away.

They realized he was helpless and enjoyed the grease off his trousers and boots and were working on the grease on his shirt when a cougar screamed from the edge of the woods. All the small animals took off just as Robert Spells was pulling wildly at his ropes but doing nothing but making the knots tighter. It looked a great deal as if he would be killed by this cougar, this puma, whatever they were called in this region. The cat was big and he came in cautiously, circling the camp, thinking that it must be a trap. Several times, he stopped and growled and screamed, showing his long teeth, the ones that would soon tear at Robert Spells's flesh.

He was sitting, swishing his tail back and forth, getting ready to pounce, when a terrible growl came from behind him. The cat jumped literally into the air and came down facing the threat from behind. It was a grizzly bear. He stood on his back legs and was over eight feet tall. He growled furiously and swatted the air with his terrible claws.

The cat wasn't about to admit that the prey belonged to the grizzly. The two of them circled each other within ten feet of one another.

———

The British captain of the rebel dragoons wasn't about to let the wagon train get away. There were too many valuables within those wagons, and the young women themselves would be good fun, then they could be sold to the surrounding tribes after they killed everyone else.

Plus, Captain Reginald Thomson held a grudge against the two mountain men. He wasn't outsmarted very often, but that move of getting the Paiutes to attack him, well, he had to admit, he was going to enjoy peeling Immanuel and Uzziah's skin off their fat bodies.

They set up an ambush about a day or two from where the Paiutes had scared them off. Captain

Thomson figured they would be relaxed enough to catch them off guard, maybe not?

———

It was early morning when the dragoons attacked from the east as the sun was coming up. The settlers, the pilgrims, screamed, and some went for their rifles, and some were killed outright.

Immanuel and Uzziah organized the defenses and fairly soon had a steady stream of fire at the dragoons, who were circling the wagons like Injuns. The Paiutes had camped elsewhere because that's what made them comfortable. They came over the rise and rode down upon the dragoons.

"Cap, we can't fight two fights at the same time," a corporal said as an arrow pierced his neck and his lifeblood ran down his chest right before he slid off his horse.

———

Immanuel and Uzziah were firing their Hawkens with deadly results, and just as the captain was making up his mind to get while the getting was good, the Paiutes swarmed in and gathered up what was left of the dragoons.

Like most encounters, the worst of the men who had planned it and gotten everyone in on it weren't harmed. Some of the dragoons were dead or wounded so badly that they wouldn't make the sunset.

The chief of the Paiutes and Immanuel had a

signing talk and the Paiute chief laughed again. Uzziah had no idea what they had cooked up.

They were close to the Dalles, taking the dragoons who had survived as prisoners. They tied them up and put them on their horses with the horses tied together, nose to tail and trailing the wagons. A guard was put on them.

They got to the cliffs around the rapids which spread out from there and on down toward the ocean about 150 miles away.

The Paiutes had brought some canoes to the spot where they were to meet Immanuel. There were ten or so canoes, and the settlers traded for them, and they got a good deal.

"What are you going to do with us?" Captain Thomson asked.

"We're gonna set ya free," Immanuel said.

The captain looked at the canoes, then down to the rapids which gathered around the Dalles.

"No, no, you can't do this," he begged Immanuel.

"Would you rather we lined you up along the tree line and shot you down?"

Captain Thomson looked at his men. They shrugged, every one of them. Being given a chance in a canoe was better than absorbing lead, that was for sure.

The men were talking rapidly as they loaded up in the canoes, and there was advice abounding about how to manipulate the rapids, and whatever nautical advice anyone had ever heard of was summarily dispersed.

When they shoved off, one of the canoes tried to pull in before the rapids, but Uzziah and Immanuel took two of them out with their Hawkens from about two hundred yards. The others threw their dead comrades out of the canoe and paddled back into the mainstream.

Uzziah, Immanuel, and Fred Trimble stood on a ridge and watched the fleet of canoes enter the first rapids.

"Are those men having fun?" Billy asked.

"We certainly hope so," Uzziah said.

"One of them tipped over," Karen said. "Look, the men are trying to swim."

Those who had capsized were dashed against rocks and even on the ridge, they could see the blood spray when their heads hit the boulders. Then, the rest of the canoes disappeared around a bend in the Columbia, heading for the worst part of the rapids.

"Do ya think any of 'em will make it?" Uzziah asked.

Immanuel looked back at the foaming rapids and the beautiful, swift-moving water and shrugged.

———

Confronting death by gunshot, or hanging, or any other sort of death was one thing, but seeing two killing machines circling each other, knowing that the winner would, with all ferocity, continue killing and you'd be the next one torn apart, well, that does something to a man.

Robert Spells, who never considered himself much without a pistol, now became Robert Spells, about to be literally torn apart while still alive. He pulled at the ropes and jerked like he was going to jerk himself away from the Ponderosa, then he realized he had enough rope to climb the tree with his back to it. He jerked the loop up higher on the tree, then digging in the heels of his boots, shimmied up the tree backward. Even from a height of fifteen feet or more, he knew he was toast as soon as the battle below had been decided.

Finally, the two giants of the Rockies threw themselves into mortal combat, and the fur was flying and the growling just about took over Robert's mind, until he remembered he still had his knife in his boot. With the slack created by the ropes stretching, he managed to just get his fingertips on the end of the knife. Twice, he almost had it, and twice, it slipped back into his boot.

At long last, as the battle below was winding down and it looked a whole lot like the puma was getting beaten, Robert got the knife totally out of his boot, but when he went to grab it better, it slipped from his fingers and began to fall to the forest floor below. In a last-ditch effort, he kicked out with his boot, which caused the rope to go slack, and as he was falling the fifteen feet to the bottom of the tree, he managed, somehow, to grab the knife, which was falling with him.

Immediately, he cut the rope just in time to see the mountain cat scurry off, leaving the grizzly. The big bear licked his wounds, and they were considerable, then turned to see his lunch. He stood on his hind legs and growled as Robert ran toward the cabin front of the cave. He slammed the door just as the bear was running toward the cabin, he threw the log over the entrance to keep the door closed, but when the bear hit the door, the log and the door exploded into a million splinters.

Robert ran toward the back of the cave where he remembered that Jedidiah had some dynamite, which he'd used to hollow the cave out for his home. He could hear the bear coming after him as he grabbed a stick of dynamite and got out his lucifer. The bear was on him and grabbing him, he threw him against the far wall of the cave. All the breath came out of Robert as the bear stood again, growling and swiping the air with his massive claws, a final show of strength. Robert lit the dynamite fuse and threw it toward the box of other dynamite sticks, maybe six others, then he sprinted toward the exit.

As he ran from the broken-down door, he could see the bear walking on his hind legs toward the entrance and that was the last thing he remembered, as the whole cave exploded outward and cast him fifty feet into the forest.

The explosion could be heard for miles, and as the smoke roiled up toward the sky, the debris rained down for the next five minutes. Robert Spells cheered himself. He'd never done that before, but he figured there was a first time for everything.

6

Captain Reginald Thomson came crawling out of the Columbia River about the same time Robert Spells rode off from Jedidiah's destroyed home. Both men had one thing and one thing only on their minds. Getting even with the bastards who had sold them to death. Immanuel James Jones and his partner now were in the sights of two men who would, if they had to, dedicate the rest of their lives to finding and killing these men.

Robert Spells saw glory in what he was going to do, and the captain just saw blood, and it was blood that both of them wanted.

———

There was no road past the Dalles to Oregon City. The Oregon Trail ended at the Cascade Mountains. Immanuel and Uzziah got to work felling trees and helping the wagons they had left in their train to make rafts to float on down to Fort Vancouver. From there, the settlers, pilgrims, could make up their own minds about which way they wanted to go.

There, at Fort Vancouver, there was a man known as the Great White Eagle, as he was called by natives. He ran the trading post for the British and was supposed to discourage emigrants from settling in the area. But the man was a Christian through and through. When settlers actually made the trip down the Columbia past the Dalles and other dangerous rapids, he could in no way find it in his heart to discourage them. In fact, nine times out of ten, he loaned them money or gave them supplies on credit. It was said at the time of his death, he was still owed many thousands of dollars, which he would never be paid.

Of course, to get the credit, those wagons had to brave the Columbia River and its many rapids. The Dalles had been avoided, but the last part of the journey seemed to be the most dangerous, and Uzziah and Immanuel weren't about to let the kids they'd rescued go it alone on this final leg of the journey.

The tree felling took the better part of three days. No one among them had ever built a raft, but with the help of the Paiutes that had rounded up the British troops—as a way of payment, Uzziah and Immanuel had made sure the Paiutes got the cavalry horses. This greatly pleased the Paiutes, and they gladly helped the settlers build the rafts.

The work was hard, but with the Paiutes' help, they had the rafts built and the day came for them to put the wagons on the rafts. A few men were selected to drive the livestock on the shore for the next eighty-three miles. Obviously, if the rafts made it to Fort Vancouver, they would be ahead of their livestock and would have to wait for their arrival.

"We can't let those young fellas take the livestock without one of us being with them," Uzziah said.

"Let me translate that. What you mean is, you ain't gonna let the black, who, by the way, follows ya around like he was your shadow—"

"That's a good name for the black horse!" Karen shouted out.

Uzziah looked at her and smiled. "You're right, it's perfect. What do you think of that, Shadow?" Uzziah asked the horse as he patted him on the neck. Shadow whinnied in appreciation. "I can't thank ye enough for naming my horse," Uzziah said to Immanuel.

"You're begging the question, the reason ya want to go with the men handling the stock is yer afraid to let *Shadow* out of yer sight. Am I right?"

"Of course, yer right. Plus, I seen what those rapids did to those dragoons."

"Yeah, me, too," Immanuel said. "But we're past the worst of them, I hope, and one of us has to take the risk with the pilgrims, and I guess it's gonna be me."

"Looks like," Uzziah said.

"Can I ride with you, Uzziah?" Karen asked.

"Won't ya miss yer brother?" Immanuel asked.

"Nah, I hope he drowns," she said, having been very annoyed with Billy recently.

"Now, Karen, ifn he does drown, how ya gonna feel?" Uzziah asked her, then he added, besides, I'm gonna go on the rafts with ya, so Immanuel can boss around those younger boys. He likes that sort of thing."

"Good," she answered without hesitating.

"Really? Truly?" Uzziah said, looking thoughtfully at her.

"Okay, I'd hate myself for wishing such a thing," she said, almost tearing up.

"Then, don't wish it," Immanuel said very practically.

"Just like that?" she asked.

"We ain't gonna remember ya said it," Uzziah assured her.

"Said what?" Immanuel chimed in.

"Good, then I take it back, I take it all back," she said and smiled.

As Immanuel took Shadow's reins, the two men exchanged glances. They knew what those glances meant. It meant that no matter how much Uzziah wanted to be with his horse, Shadow, his real responsibility was to those two kids. Sometimes, what you want gets in the way of what you have to do.

———

Having regained his strength from catching salmon and staying away from the bears who were also hunting them, Captain Thomson was almost one hundred percent. Now, all he needed was a gun or two and a horse.

He started hiking west because he believed that he was more than likely going to come upon a settler's cabin. He was right. He had hiked for less than two days when he saw smoke curling from a log cabin. He sat in the woods where no one could see him and watched for the better part of two days. In those two days, he learned there were three people in the cabin. A man, his good-looking wife, and a tiny baby. He pondered how he might go about taking what he wanted from them, and the pondering stopped when, early the next morning, the young man kissed his wife and the baby goodbye and headed somewhere on his horse.

The captain waited for an hour. If a person forgets something they had intended to take with them, they would come back if they were less than an hour away, but more than an hour, it wasn't likely.

When he snuck up on the woman, she was hanging clothes on the clothesline that ran between the house and a big tree. The clothes were dripping wet, well, she had tried to wring them out, but she was small and didn't have much strength in her arms. The captain liked that because it meant that she would be no trouble when it came time for him to take what he wanted both from her and from the cabin.

When he touched her shoulders at the clothesline, she laughed and turned to him as if he were her husband. Well, in a way, he was about to be.

She screamed when she saw that it wasn't her husband who had returned for a poke, but a total stranger. He didn't much care for women screaming, and with one punch, he put her out.

The baby was setting in a basket, which he imagined at times she used for various things. It wasn't awake and the scream of its mother hadn't awakened it.

He stripped the woman, who, it turned out, was very shapely, and tied her legs to the posts on the bed and her arms to the other posts. He was so turned on by seeing her naked that he didn't even wait for her to wake up, he just mounted up and had a ride. Halfway through the poke, which she seemed to be enjoying by the moans she was making, she woke up and started screaming again. He knocked her out and was finishing off inside her when a man entered the cabin. It was the woman's husband.

"What the hell!" he screamed as he sat the basket down with the baby in it and drew his revolver.

The captain struggled to get off the woman when the gun her husband was holding went off. The shot went wide of its mark and creased the left side of the captain. He tumbled off the bed, screaming.

The husband cocked his piece again, but something went wrong. It was the one thing every man hated—misfire!

The two men, one without pants on and bleeding profusely from his side, the other trying to keep the fight away from the awakened and screaming baby boy in the basket. They wrestled around the cabin, knocking things off shelves, nearly running into the stove, when the captain picked up one of the fireplace implements and cold-cocked the husband over the head. He went down, but he wasn't out.

The captain grabbed his pants, gun, and holster and ran for the door, which was opened.

The husband struggled for a bit, then staggered to his feet, grabbed the shotgun off the mantle, ran to the door, and took a shot at the captain. He was too far away and galloping too fast for the buckshot to do him any harm.

He went to the barn, where they had a couple of other animals. A milk cow, which the man had milked that morning, and a horse, if you could call it that. The horse had seen better days, to say the least. The man who was raping his wife had jumped on the husband's horse to get away fast, so he saddled the old boy up and put a bridle on him. The old gelding seemed excited, he hadn't been taken for a ride in some time. He was going to chase that murdering scum down on a very old horse.

He went back into the cabin and his wife was crying. He untied her, they hugged, then she went to her baby and grabbed him up. She covered herself with one of the blankets.

"Well, don't just stand there, go after that bastard!" she screamed at him, and he was out the door, throwing himself up on the old horse.

The trail was fresh and he could recognize his horses' prints anywhere.

———

Robert Spells was making his way down the mountain on the horse he'd ridden into the wagon train camp. Well, at least the old man had kept his horse for him. He rounded a bend in the path, and there was Jedidiah, riding up toward his cabin. The old man looked up just in time to be surprised.

"What the—" was all he got out before Robert blew a hole in his chest. The old man grabbed at his wound as he slid off the horse. Spells, thinking it might be a good idea to have another horse, tied the reins to the horse Jedidiah was riding to the D-ring on his saddle and left the dying man on the trail.

"Yer a no-good, law hound, and I wish ya nothin' but bad luck, son," he yelled, but Spells was already down the trail and couldn't make out exactly what the old man was harping about.

About halfway through the first set of rapids, Uzziah knew he'd taken the wrong choice. He should have gone with the livestock. These maybe weren't as bad as the ones Immanuel had consigned the dragoons to, but they were hell on water, that's for sure.

He could hear the men on the various rafts screaming instructions to those who had the long poles, which the Paiutes said would help guide them down through the rapids, but he should have known what was awaiting them when the Paiutes took the dragoons' horses and traveled back to their camp, not wanting to help navigate the rafts.

Uzziah saw one raft in front of him explode on a huge boulder. Everything that family had owned—it wasn't the Trimbles, and he was glad for that—all their earthly belongings went skyward and then sank beneath the raging waters. He saw two people go under and grabbed the arm of a woman who was bobbing in the water when they flashed by. She was nearly drowned but stayed on the bottom of the raft, coughing as Uzziah angled to avoid the killer boulder.

No other wagons were lost, and the next few rapids were bad, but not like that first set, or maybe he'd just gotten used to it. In any case, the four wagons made it through all the rapids and were gliding nicely in calm waters toward Fort Vancouver.

———

Captain Thomson, wounded and still bleeding, was making his way toward Fort Vancouver. He figured if the mountain men helped the wagon train all the way, they would end up in that place before they let the settlers go their own way. As he rode toward the Columbia, he could hear the roar of the rapids, which had destroyed all of his dragoons except himself. It was true, he had broken from the ranks of those who followed His Majesty's Army Code, but this was America, and things didn't work by rules. If you wanted something in this god-forsaken country, you simply took it. And now, when he found those two bastards who had sent himself and his men to their deaths on the river, well, he was going to take their lives.

"Oh my God," he said, in spite of the fact that he needed to be quiet.

Below him, following the Columbia, was one of the mountain men, the one who had the idea about putting them into the Paiute canoes and sending them to their deaths. There he was, Immanuel James Jones. He was traveling with two other men, and they were all well-armed. They had the livestock from the remaining wagons, and obviously, they were traveling to Fort Vancouver so the settlers could hook up their wagons again and finally end their journey.

There were three of them and only one of him, so he decided to follow quietly. He would hang back, and when they reached Fort Vancouver, he would find an opportunity to get the two mountain men by themselves and dispatch them at the same time.

———

Robert Spells, the Pinkerton Agent, was lost. He was from Chicago, and as he tried to remember which side of a tree moss grew on, he kept on ending back up where he recognized he had started. In his frustration and annoyance, he screamed at the horses with him but would not give the horse he was riding his head, which would have allowed the animal to find the Oregon Trail on his own. But like so many people who are lost, they keep thinking they can find their way out and compound their plight by taking charge and pulling the horse away from where it knew it needed to be. It would be a while before Immanuel or Uzziah were in harm's way from this city slicker.

———

When the livestock finally made it to Fort Vancouver, the wagons had been waiting for some time. The men who knew their oxen and horses ran toward the group with harnesses and bridles. Fairly soon after Immanuel and Uzziah had been reunited and they were swapping stories, the wagons were again with the animals who would pull them down to Oregon City. The man who the British had running the fort, John McLoughlin, had procured land south of the fort in Oregon City. It was the first American settlement in the Willamette Valley and contrary to what the British wanted, McLoughlin actually helped the settlement of Oregon by the Americans.

The pilgrims had been waiting too long to get underway, so they all headed south. Billy and Karen came running up to the two mountain men.

"Aren't ya gonna go with us!?" Billy asked Immanuel.

"No, son, our job is done here. We're headed back to our mountains," Immanuel said.

Karen simply pulled herself up on the black with Uzziah by using the black's mane. She hugged Uzziah and he didn't know what to do. Fairly soon, the parade of wagons brought Trimble's wagon alongside where the mountain men were mounted.

"Children, if yer comin' with us, ya better get onboard," Fred Trimble said.

"Go on, and be a good boy," Immanuel told Billy, who reached up and shook his hand as if he were all grown up.

Karen slipped off Shadow and kissed him on the face.

"Bye, Shadow, it was great to get to know you," she said.

The two children ran toward the back of the Trimbles wagon. Billy jumped up, and gave a hand to Karen when she ran up behind him. They settled themselves in the back of the wagon and continued to wave to Uzziah and Immanuel.

The two big, old mountain men were silently weeping. Immanuel turned to Uzziah.

"Ya say a thing 'bout this to anyone, I'll skin ya alive!"

"Wagh!" Uzziah screamed and took off on Shadow, daring Immanuel to keep up.

Immanuel's horse took off after Shadow. The people along the fort road shouted at them for their excessive speed, but they didn't slow down.

Captain Thomson had had his wound seen to by a doctor and paid him the last of his stolen money. As he came out of the doctor's office, the two mountain men rode by like the wind.

Well, he couldn't exactly jump on the horse he'd stolen and gallop out of town. Everyone would have noticed, and when those two ended up dead, they might remember him as the one who was chasing them. He mounted up and rode easily out of town. He'd catch up with them, and when he did, he'd have his revenge.

He followed them in the foothills and stayed off the ridges so he couldn't be seen. He spent two nights trailing them before he decided to take them on.

It was the morning of the third day when he snuck into their camp. Uzziah had gotten up to pee when he saw him squatting by the embers that used to be their fire.

"Shhh!" the captain said as he placed his index finger in front of his lips.

"I gotta pee," Uzziah whispered.

"Go right where yer at."

Uzziah turned away from Captain Thomson and let go a mighty stream of piss.

"Hey!" Immanuel protested from his bedroll, "Take that junk away from camp."

"Good morning, Immanuel," the captain said. Immanuel was reaching for his weapon when Thomson held up the gun he was looking for.

———

Uzziah fixed breakfast for all three of them, and they got on the trail again. Thomson had been dreaming about what he was going to do long before they got to the cliffs over the Dalles. He had both men pick out rocks, which he tied them to, then they walked carrying their rocks to the edge of the cliff.

"Just wish I had canoes to send ya down the rapids in, but this will do," he said as he pointed his gun at Immanuel. Just as Immanuel was about to be shot, another shot rang out and a strange expression came over the captain's face. He turned to see who had shot him, and there stood the husband of the woman he'd raped.

"Die, ya bastard!" the husband said and fired three more shots into the captain's body.

They got themselves untied with the help of the man who had killed the captain. He asked if there was anything else he could do for them, and if there wasn't, he was headed back to his cabin. They said their goodbyes.

Uzziah dragged the body of the captain up to the edge of the cliff and they tied the two rocks on it and pushed it over. It bounced and flopped its way to the Columbia, where it sunk and was not seen again.

7

They rode easy back to the mountains, and once within their sheltering presence, they felt as if they were home again. It was the morning of the third day back into the Rockies that they heard swearing and a loud man's voice. They snuck up on the man who was beating a horse. Something that no western man ever let happen.

"You stupid, no-good, son of a jackass!" he yelled at the horse and was raising the quirt up and about to hit the horse across the face when the quirt was shot from his hand.

"Damn!" he said as he grabbed his right hand, which was bleeding badly.

"They didn't teach ya Pinkertons any better than that," Immanuel said.

"I'm lost," Spells said as he wrapped his bandana around his shot-up hand.

They tied him up and put him back on the horse he was beating, and the other horse followed.

They were less than a mile from where Robert

Spells shot Jedidiah. When they rounded the bend where he'd shot him, Spells braced himself, but there was no body. They rode on up to what remained of Jedidiah's place.

"Holy hog wart!" Uzziah said, and Immanuel simply whistled.

An Injun pony was tied in what remained of the barn, and there was a campfire built and bacon in the pan. Fairly soon, Rose Water walked from the wreckage of the cabin. If she was surprised to see them, she did not look like it.

"Good, you here help me with Jed," she said.

The old man was bound up with herbs that Rose had wrapped around his body. He looked none the worse for wear. When he saw Spells, he started cussing.

"Give me a gun, I'm gonna kill this son of a bitch!" he yelled, then he grabbed his side and yelled out in pain.

"See what I mean. Every time I get him settled, he does something to hurt himself," Rose complained.

They stayed there a few days until Jedidiah was able to ride.

"You and Rose Water will stay with us this winter. There's too much work to be done on yer place, we'll fix it next spring. In the meantime, you and Rose can stay in one of the cabins," Immanuel said.

"I paid her in advance for some pokes, and that's why she showed up, to honor my payment. Don't ever let me hear ya say ya can't trust no Injuns. This Injun whore is as good as her word," Jedidiah said as they placed him up on his horse.

———

They rode back to the three cabins. There was a discussion about what to do with Spells.

"We should let him go," Uzziah argued.

"That varmint like to have been the end of me," Jedidiah spat out.

"Yeah, well, we been chased out here because of something that Uzziah and I did—"

"So, ya did kill that undersheriff!" Spells had been eavesdropping.

"The question is, do we want another law dog notch on our guns?" Immanuel whispered.

"He can't find his way outta a gunny sack. I say we blindfold him, give him a gun and knife, supplies, and take him far enough down the trail. Hell, we'll find him next spring froze to death," Uzziah suggested.

Jedidiah and Immanuel looked at each other and grinned, both men liked the idea.

"I can give him a goodbye poke," Rose said, and all three men nodded in agreement.

When Spells got off Rose Water, they put him on his horse, gave him some supplies, an old gun, a knife, and blindfolded him after they'd tied his hands to the saddle horn.

"What's the big idea? How am I supposed to see?"

"Yer not," Uzziah said, "I'm riding you down the hill and a piece, then we's gonna let ya go."

"It's a trick," Spells yelled.

"Ifn ya come back this way, we will shoot ya on sight," Immanuel said.

"Ya can bet on it!" Jedidiah said.

Uzziah led Spells, blindfolded and his hands tied to the saddle horn, about ten miles from their camp. He did some things like circle around and come back the same way a couple of times, just in case Spells got his sense of direction back, which they were sure he never had.

When they finally stopped, the sun was low and it was almost night. Uzziah took the blindfold off and untied Spells's hands.

"You go fer yer gun, I'll kill ya right here," Uzziah said, and Spells blinked hard since he hadn't seen anything all day.

"I'm gonna come back with other agents. We'll round you bastards up if it's the last thing we do," Spells yelled at Uzziah as he rode off.

———

They spent the winter, which was a hard one, in the cabins which Immanuel had built. Jedidiah insisted on helping with the traps in the spring when the pelts would be thicker and richer. Everything was going well until he came down with a cold, which must have turned into pneumonia. He suffered something awful and was having trouble breathing.

"I ain't gonna go out without a final poke," he told them that night after supper.

"You too sick, old man," Rose said, then she saw the looks on Uzziah and Immanuel's faces. "But maybe can ride one more time," she said and helped Jedidiah back to the cabin with the pot-bellied stove in it.

"Ya think he's dying?" Uzziah asked Immanuel.

"Well, hell yes, he's dying, ifn his lungs get any more water in 'em he'll drown hisself."

They were sitting out by the big fire which they'd built to warm the old man, and they could hear Rose's ministrations to him. It sounded as if they were doing okay till Rose screamed.

Both mountain men rushed in, and Rose was still mounted on him, but she had her face covered with her hands.

"Dead man's Johnson," was all she said, and they realized that Jedidiah had kicked off while he was still in her, and his member must still be erect. They grabbed her from both sides and pulled her off the man. His member shrank when the cold air hit it, and Rose ran from the cabin crying.

———

The ground was still too hard for digging, so they put Jedidiah on top of one of the cabins. They didn't tell Rose what they had done with him.

"Where his body?" she kept asking.

"We done told ya, it's safe till spring, when we'll bury the old cuss."

———

The winter hung on well into spring, and they didn't think the thaw was ever going to come. When it did, they got the surprise of their lives.

"I in family way," Rose announced one morning in late spring.

The two men looked at her, and she knew their minds.

"Not yours or yours," she said, pointing to the two men in succession.

"How do ya know?" Uzziah asked politely.

"The man who died while in me sent his soul into me with jizum," she said with a straight face.

Immanuel and Uzziah just looked at each other and shrugged. Sometimes, when an Injun got a notion, there was no dispelling it.

"So, it's the man who died. It's his baby?" Immanuel asked.

"The man who died will be reborn from me," she said and caressed her belly.

———

They were going down to the early Spring Rendezvous. Rose Water's belly was as big as they'd ever seen a woman's belly. She rode anyway, said she'd seen her own mother do it with her last sister.

When they were almost off the mountain they lived on, and there was plenty of snow still around, they came upon a body.

It was the Pinkerton Agent, Robert Spells.

"Well, I'll be, ya was right!" Immanuel said, looking at Uzziah, "The son of a gun didn't make it off the mountain."

They prodded him with their Hawkens and he was frozen solid. He looked peaceful, though, like he'd come to terms with his death, who knew? The horse he'd been riding was nowhere to be seen, and they imagined it had headed for the plains, the place the horse would have gladly taken Mr. Spells if he'd have let her.

Rose Water would not look at Spells, she didn't like the fact his eyes had frozen open and it looked as if he was looking at them.

They left Spells right where he'd frozen to death

and figured by the time they got back from Rendezvous, the critters would have taken care of him.

———

The rendezvous were getting smaller every year, and the mountain men who did come were disappointed that Rose Water was no longer a whore. She had decided to raise up the soul of Jedidiah after it came out of her body as a baby. They all laughed about that when she told them that, but they all crossed themselves when they left her presence. Sometimes, men can be afraid of the strangest things.

One night, when everyone was up late, and they all had been drinking up the money they'd gotten from the Hudson Bay Company man, there was a scream in the night. There were about twenty mountain men around a great bonfire, and no one spoke.

"It's the soul of Jedidiah being born," someone joked, and there was a bit of laughter, then another scream.

Immanuel and Uzziah ran back to where they knew Rose was staying in the lean-to they had fashioned. Sure enough, she was in labor.

———

The labor went on for almost a day, and both men took turns placing wet rags on her head and talking to her. She was nearly exhausted when the baby came out. Uzziah had helped his own father with the birthing of his last siblings, and when he let the baby finally fall into his hands, and he raised it up and spanked it hard, and it cried, Immanuel got up and backed away.

"What's wrong?" Uzziah asked.

"Take a good look at that baby," was all Immanuel said.

Uzziah held the baby toward the fire in the lean-to and nearly dropped it.

"I told ya, soul of Jedidiah born in baby," Rose said, and she took the baby, which resembled the old man so much that if they'd glued hair on its face, he would have looked just like him.

———

The next morning, when all the others came by and looked at that baby, you'd have thought Rose Water had given birth to the savior. Men were kneeling down and praying. Men who hadn't prayed in years found their God again right where they left him. Then, the parade of gifts began. It was like there were forty wise men instead of three. She had all kinds of stuff laid down there in front of her and the baby. One man even carved the name of Jesus in a plank of wood he found and gave it to her. She liked that one a lot.

Immanuel and Uzziah had never seen a rendezvous break up so suddenly. There was plenty of whiskey left and other whores who the men were enjoying, but it only took one look and the bringing of the gifts, then they were gone from camp. Immanuel figured remembering God the way they did, they also remembered something they had told God they were going to do, and the early exits were them on their way to do just those things.

Uzziah went around and scavenged the stuff that some of the mountain men had left on their hasty retreats.

Immanuel, in the meantime, had grown sufficiently accustomed to the baby—and the idea that it might, indeed, be old Jedidiah's soul reborn—that he started calling it Two-Jay.

Rose liked the name because there had been a couple of jaybirds in the trees the morning, she first fed Two-Jay. Both Uzziah and Immanuel decided she would return with them back to the cabins.

They left for the cabins once they thought that Rose could ride. They had a tiny travois set up behind her horse, and when the baby cried, she halted her horse, unwrapped Two-Jay, and fed him. It took a lot longer to get back to the cabins with all the feeding stops, but when they finally arrived, they were all relieved to be there.

8

A few months later, they found Rose dead in her cabin. There was a lot of blood, which had come from the place she liked to be poked. Two-Jay was awake and gurgling when they found her stiff body. But how would they feed the small infant?

Immanuel remembered that the man who had killed Captain Thomson had told him that the captain had raped his wife, and they had a small baby. It was a common practice back then to let babies nurse up until they were nearly four years old.

The next day, a warm one, they bound the baby up and Uzziah tied it to his back like a papoose, and they rode to where the man had said he lived.

It took them a couple of days, and by the time they found the cabin of the man, Two-Jay was crying so hard that the man, his wife, and their son, who was now walking, could hear them for miles.

The man was chopping firewood, and he stopped, recognizing the two men whose lives he'd saved. The woman could only hear the sound of a hungry baby, and when she emerged from the cabin, there were splotches of milk appearing on her dress.

Uzziah got down and she untied the crying baby and took it into the cabin. Within moments, Two-Jay had stopped crying.

"Well, why should I be surprised," the farmer had said when he was shaking hands with both the mountain men.

"Guess you know why we came by," Uzziah said, not offering any more information.

"Guess I do. Where'd the kid come from?"

"She was the squaw of a friend of ours. He died shortly after getting her pregnant, and she died a couple days ago," Immanuel explained.

"Come on in, let's get some coffee," the man suggested. "By the way, I'm Oscar Blanchard."

"Immanuel, and this is my partner, Uzziah."

Inside, they sat with coffee at the table, and the woman, her name was Ophelia, was nursing a very happy Two-Jay.

"How do you know these men?" she asked Oscar.

"He saved our lives," Uzziah told her.

"Oh my, these are the two that that madman was going to kill?"

"Yeah, hon, they are."

"And the baby, by the way, he's adorable, reminds me of my cousin Charlie when he was a little guy," Ophelia said.

"That's weird. That's the baby's name, Charles Water," Immanuel said, lying. He knew that they'd be more likely to keep the kid if they had a slight connection to him, maybe the name would be enough.

"You're kidding?" she said, looking down at the new Charlie Water.

"There's nothin' 'bout that boy that hasn't been different," Uzziah admitted.

She kept looking down at the boy. "He's so cute," she said, then realized something. "You can't feed him, can you?" she asked, looking at the two mountain men.

"Not since his ma died, no," Uzziah said, hoping against hope.

"Oscar?" was all she said.

He looked at her, then back down to the coffee in his cup.

"He'd have a brother," Oscar said.

Ophelia got up and came over to her husband and hugged him while still nursing. The towel fell away, exposing her ample breast. Both mountain men saw, but looked away, being the gentlemen they were.

"You said she was a squaw, but he don't look Injun," Oscar said.

"He is," Immanuel said. "I think she was Cherokee." Immanuel didn't have a clue what tribe Rose was, but he'd always like the name of that tribe, Cherokee.

"His pa was a friend of ours, Jedidiah Smith," Uzziah made up Jedidiah's last name, they were winging this whole thing.

———

They accepted the invitation to stay for supper. After Ophelia had put Charlie down for a nap and put her own son, Will, in charge of watching him, she started fixing the meal for all of them. Uzziah and Immanuel helped Oscar with some chores that it took two or more men to do. He had made the barn bigger but hadn't put on the roof. They got part of it put up when Ophelia called them in for supper.

The meal was simple enough, venison steaks, but she had chicken-fried them, dipped them into egg/milk, then dropped them into flour with salt and pepper mixed in. They were fantastic, and Uzziah had watched her with the last of the venison, and he would use the same recipe later when they were back on the mountain.

The two mountain men stayed for a week and not only were able to help Oscar finish the barn roof, but they also helped him finish pigeon lofts in one corner of the barn. Oscar had about fifteen of these rollers, that's what he called them.

Uzziah liked the way they cooed and the noises they made when they were in their lofts. He'd take his afternoon nap by the lofts so he could go to sleep hearing them being sociable in there.

"Why do they call 'em tumblers?" Uzziah asked one afternoon.

"I'll show ya," Oscar said, and he let them all out, and they took off looking like they were never going to come back. As they gathered in the sky over their settlement, a couple of them would somersault backward, fall thirty feet or so, then just start flying again.

"Whoa!" Uzziah exclaimed. "Why do they do that?"

"Well, lots of speculation about why, but I think they do it to fool predators, even men. Imagine ya'd shot at that group of pigeons, wouldn't ya have thought ya got one?"

"Yeah, yeah, you're right," Uzziah said as he looked at them circling the settlement, and a couple of them tumbled again. "That is so amazing."

———

The day they left to go back to the cabins, Will was playing with Charlie in his little cradle, which Will had used until he got bigger.

Once again, the two grizzly mountain men found themselves mounted up and saying goodbye to friends. Uzziah looked over to Immanuel, who seemed to be wiping something from his eye, and he grinned through his own tears.

"Here, we want ya to take these two rollers with ya," Oscar said as he tied a small cage on the back of Uzziah's saddle. Now, when ya get to where yer goin', just feed them for a couple of days and give 'em plenty of water, then let 'em go. They'll come back here, and if I ever have to send a message to you two, I'll send one of these. Be a good idea to build them a loft while they're there, so they can be in it a while before ya let 'em go."

"Thank you, folks, so much. Rose and Jedidiah Smith would be so pleased to know that Charlie found himself a good home," Uzziah said, and looking at Immanuel, who couldn't speak, they kicked their horses up and rode west.

They had ridden for a couple of hours before either one of them said a word. Uzziah kept turning around and looking at the rollers, who seemed to be doing fine riding behind him.

"What's this about us getting involved with all these kids?" Immanuel asked.

"Babies," Uzziah said. "Maybe we're gettin' trained up for one of our own?"

Immanuel looked at him and he was not smiling. "I'd ride after you and kick you off yer hoss, but shadow can run faster than any horse I ever seen."

———

They'd thrown Rose up on the snow-covered roof of her cabin along with Jedidiah. By the time they got back, it had all but thawed up at the cabins. They brought the bloated bodies down and poked holes in them to let out the gases. They were wearing their bandana when they rolled Jedidiah and Rose into the same grave.

After they'd covered them up, both took off their bandanas and stood there.

"Seems like we been buryin' or killin' a lot of folks lately," Uzziah said.

"Ya think? I don't know what to make of it all, do ya?"

"Well, life goes on, and my guess is, we been on both sides of that conundrum and may likely be on it again soon," Uzziah said thoughtfully.

———

The first thing Uzziah did was build a loft for the pigeons. He put it close to his window in the cabin he liked so he could hear them cooing when he was lying down to sleep. He fed them good and put a little water trough in there, which they seemed to enjoy.

221

They had taken the traps up before they left with Two-Jay, and now, Uzziah went one way and Immanuel the other, and they reset all the traps to get the prime spring pelts.

When Uzziah got to his first set of traps, they weren't hidden the way they had left them. Someone had baited them with castor, sank them down in the pond, and secured them really well. Someone was using them as their own. He decided he'd wait till later in the day, when whoever was using their traps would show up to take the pelts.

He'd fallen asleep. It was later, the sun had moved from one side of his face, where he lay, to the other. He could hear someone in the pond talking to themself.

"He's a big 'un," a female voice said. No one spoke back to her, so Uzziah figured she was remarking to herself the way folks have a tendency to do when they think they're alone.

He moved ever so slightly, turning his head so he could see through the brush he was lying in. She was young, maybe thirty, maybe not. Her reddish-blond hair sent strobes of light to his eyes and he smiled. Beautiful hair. She had on jeans with suspenders, and big old boots, and a floppy hat which suited her. She wasn't tall, nor was she short. She had a nice face, and Uzziah wondered what he was going to do. He was about to move when a man's voice broke through the afternoon shadows.

"How many have ya got?" he asked.

He came into Uzziah's point of view and was older than the girl, much older, perhaps her father?

As they were gathering what she'd collected so far and putting them on the pack mule that the man had brought with him, Uzziah figured that the older man must have taken his pelts from the traps Immanuel went to set again.

The old geezer had a Greener strapped to his back and a couple of other guns set here and there in his belt. He was an armory of weapons, and he had a knife or two. Uzziah decided to follow them and find their camp before he went and got Immanuel.

———

When he got back to the cabins, Immanuel was sitting outside, carving on a stick.

"Did you find what I found?" he asked Uzziah as he rode up.

"Sure did, and I found their camp," Uzziah said, and within two minutes, both men were riding for the southern slope of the same mountain they lived on.

———

It was late by the time they got to the camp. Uzziah had filled Immanuel in. Two people, one a young girl and the other a grizzled old man, who was most likely her pa. The fire they had built up said they were afraid of letting people know they were there. It was barely big enough to make coffee over.

"Hello, the camp!" Immanuel shouted out. Uzziah hadn't dreamed this was the way his partner was going to deal with this situation.

Guns were cocked, and the girl dropped back into the shadows.

"Come on in," the old man had said. It was the

Code of the West that a traveler could not be turned away from a friendly fire, if indeed it was a friendly fire.

They rode in and knew that, behind them, the girl had her guns pointed at them. They dismounted and stood beside the fire.

The old man looked them over and realized they weren't strangers to these parts.

"Grab a cup, we got coffee," the old man said.

"We?" Uzziah said, and he could see the disappointment on the man's face for letting them know someone else was around.

"Come on in, Leah," he said, the disappointment dripping from his voice.

She walked in as if she had been behind her friend the whole time, but both Uzziah and Immanuel had heard her breaking twigs as she circled back to where her *father*? stood.

Both of them had their guns on the two mountain men.

"Are ya gonna let us have coffee or aeriate us?"

"I ain't sure what that means?" the older man said.

"He wants to know if we're gonna let him drink or make him a sieve?"

The old man laughed some, a good hearty laugh, then he stopped and cocked the Greener.

Both Uzziah and Immanuel tensed up some, but nothing that those two could tell. They had made some assumptions about these two. They were probably from down on the plains and came up here to avoid the law. There were many a mountain man who began his career that way. But what they couldn't figure out was why he'd brought the girl with him.

"Them traps is your'n, ain't they?" the man asked.

"I'm Immanuel James Jones, and this here is my partner, Uzziah Ferguson O'Bannon, and yes, the traps you're using..." He gestured toward the pile of pelts that were not curing, just stacked on one another and rotting. "And it looks like you've done well in the last month, but them pelts are ruined, and ya won't get nothin' fer 'em at any trading post."

"How'd ya know about the trading post?" the old man asked, and the Greener swung around toward them again.

"Didn't until ya told us," Immanuel said.

"Damn!" the old man said.

"It's okay, papa," Leah said as she touched his arm.

"Are ya bounty hunters?" the old man asked.

"Not hardly," Uzziah said, then added, "Why, ya got a bounty on ya?"

"Papa, we can't kill these men, they haven't done nothin' to us," Leah said and meant it.

"I know," he said as he lowered the Greener, and slumped down by the fire.

"I kilt my boyfriend," Leah said.

"Why?" Immanuel asked.

"He was not a good man," she said.

"He beat the living shit out of her," the old man said.

"Better that he's dead then, can't cotton no man that hits a woman, especially one as purty as you," Uzziah said, and Immanuel looked over at his partner, thinking, *Are ya tryin' to make trouble?'"

"Let's ease on down here beside the fire and have some coffee, what do ya say?" Immanuel asked.

9

It ain't every day that a woman killed a man, but it wasn't unheard of. Theodore Blacksmith told them the entire story. He had warned the boyfriend to stop beating up on his daughter, but the man continued. He was rich and he thought a part of riches was being able to hit up on any woman that liked him. At first, it seemed that Leah Blacksmith would get this one to marry her, and that kept the old man at bay a bit. But the last time she'd come home all beat up, he went berserk. She followed him to her boyfriend's house, an almost mansion down near the river and the trading post. He didn't know she was there, and when he was all squared off with Mr. Beater, and she knew her pa was going to be outdrawn, she had hidden up and drygulched her boyfriend before he could kill her pa.

"I still think I coulda beat him to the draw," Theodore Blacksmith said.

"No, Pa, ya couldn't have. That's what I've been tryin' to tell ya. He was fast as lightning."

"He's rottin' fast now," the old man said and chuckled.

There was a scrambling from the bushes and a voice rose up above everything else.

"This is Jean Baptiste Charbonneau, and my posse from Fort Vrain have ya surrounded, and ifn ya don't surrender, we'll take you by force," a deep voice with the twinge of an accent said.

"Shit!" exclaimed Theodore.

Immanuel had the coffee pot in his hand when the man had shouted out. He threw it on the small fire and all four of them, by instinct, rolled away from the fire in different directions.

Guns were being fired, and bullets were stripping the leaves off trees and bushes as Uzziah grabbed both reins and led their horses out of harm's way. He couldn't see Immanuel but nearly ran into him as he was getting ready to mount up. The firing was still concentrated on the camp of the Blacksmiths.

"You were gonna leave me, weren't ya?" Immanuel whispered to Uzziah.

"Get on yer damned horse and let's get the hell outta here," Uzziah said, then he saw that Immanuel had Leah's hand in his.

"Put her up on Shadow with you, and ride fer our camp. I'll find the old man and meet you back there," Immanuel said, then disappeared into the brush.

There was more gunfire as Uzziah rode away with Leah holding onto his considerable waist and trying to stay on as Shadow showed off his speed through the trees.

"How does he keep from hitting a tree?" she asked.

"Don't have the foggiest, but keep yer head down,

he don't consider how much is on top of him." And sure enough, they ducked just in time to have a branch slip over their heads instead of taking them off.

————

They made it back to the cabins fairly quickly. Uzziah did not build up a fire out front but lit the pot-bellied stove for heat, and they sat in the room where Rose Water had died. Uzziah tried not to think about it.

"I'm worried about my pa," Leah said.

"Yeah, I understand, but ya have no idea how slick Immanuel can be."

"Well, he sure got me outta there without a problem."

"Then, he'll bring yer pa to ya, have no worry."

"What ya keep these pigeons fer, ya gonna eat 'em?"

"No, they belong to a friend of ours. They're homin' pigeons," Uzziah tried to explain, but you could tell Leah was having trouble understanding. He guessed she'd never heard of such a thing but was too embarrassed to ask.

She went to sleep in the rocker next to the stove. The pigeons were cooing in the background. He covered her with a blanket, the one which had covered Rose Water's body after she'd died, but she didn't know that.

————

It was several hours later that Uzziah heard horses coming into their camp. He cocked his pistols and slipped outside. It was Immanuel and Theodore Blacksmith.

"He's been hit, we got to get the bullets out of him," Immanuel said as he dismounted and helped Theodore off his horse.

"Oh, oh, oh," Theodore complained as he was helped off his horse.

"Did ya lose the Frenchman?"

"What'd ya think?" Immanuel offered, "Ya know how famous that man is?"

"No," Uzziah said as they took the old man into one of the other cabins and lit a fire.

"Don't matter, I'll tell ya later. Let's get this hombre fixed up."

They laid him on the table, and his legs drooped off the end. Immanuel threw water on him and washed off the entry wounds. He then, with the old man moaning, turned him over.

"Ya see, he's got two wounds which are through and through, ain't worried about those, as long as we can get the bleeding to staunch. It's this one here that worries me," he said, sticking his finger into the hole, and the old man screamed.

"Easy, old man," Immanuel said. "I had to see just how far that bullet had gone in," he said, then he turned to Uzziah. "Bring me my saddlebags."

Once the saddlebags were there, Immanuel dumped them on a chair. He found his scalpel and forceps.

"Where'd ya get those?" Uzziah asked him.

"Off a dead doctor, and no, I didn't kill him," Immanuel said.

A sleepy-looking Leah was at the doorway.

"Is he dead?" she asked as she walked over.

"No, he's passed out, and that's good. Uzziah sticks that scalpel and forceps into the fire for a moment, will ya?"

The girl seemed like she was a seasoned gal, she just held her pa's hand and didn't 'cause them any trouble.

Theodore woke up and smiled at his daughter. "Hey, hon, how ya doin'?"

"Better when you're better," she said, gripping his hand harder, "I love ya, Pa."

"I know, sweetheart, I know."

"What happened to the posse? Did ya kill 'em all?" she asked Immanuel.

"Don't have to kill when you can avoid. We avoided."

"But some bullets found my pa."

"Looks like, now, give me those instruments, Uzziah. Do ya drink whiskey, Mr. Blacksmith?"

"Do I!?"

"Here, tip this skyward and take as much as ya can."

The old man nearly emptied the bottle before he brought it down.

"Papa, easy," Leah said.

"No, let him. This is gonna hurt," Immanuel said.

Leah leaned against his knees, which were the last thing on the table in that direction. Uzziah grabbed both his arms and held them over the old man's head. Immanuel picked up a twig near the fire.

"Stick this in your mouth," he told the old man, whose eyes were glazing over from all the booze.

Immanuel took the scalpel, cut the wound open on

both sides, and opened it up, then dug down with the extractor forceps.

The old man was screaming with the stuck in his mouth and thrashing about, but they were holding him steady. Immanuel probed with them until he hit something that wasn't soft. That had to be the bullet, he grabbed it with the forceps and pulled it slowly out of his body. It was almost pristine, a complete bullet, not a fragment.

"Good, good," he said as he tried to show Theodore, but the stick had slipped from his mouth when he'd passed out.

———

His daughter, Leah, had sat up with him all night. They poured the rest of that bottle of whiskey on Theodore's wounds and bound them all up. Immanuel had some echinacea leaves that he stuck down inside each wound, entrance, exit, and the one he'd dug the bullet out of.

When they came into that cabin in the morning, Leah was asleep and the old man was breathing deeply. They went back outside.

Breakfast was on the fire. Uzziah had built an almost smokeless fire to cook with.

"Yer gettin' smart in yer old age, ain't ya?" Immanuel asked him. Uzziah looked up to his partner and smiled.

"Yer probably wonderin' ifn we'll ever settle into just being up here?" Immanuel asked his partner.

"Nah, I figure this is part of being up here. I imagine sometimes it's calm and others it's like this," Uzziah said, stirring the bacon so it wouldn't burn.

"I was telling ya 'bout Jean Baptiste."

"The man who is after Theodore and Leah?"

"Yeah, him. He's the son of Sacajawea, born during the Lewis and Clark Expedition."

"You're kidding?"

"Nope. He was educated by Merriweather Clark at some school back east, then spent six years in some castle in Germany, the guest of some baron. My guess is he's back. The governor of the territory granted them permission to start a trading post. I've taken my furs there only once. Had to miss Rendezvous like when I came all the way to St. Louis and met you. It must be that Jean Baptiste is running security for the post. We're gonna hafta talk to Leah about what happened there."

"I'll talk to her," Uzziah said, interested in what she would have to say.

"It seems like the good old days are over up here. We might hafta find a better spot."

"But what about yer cabins?"

"It's gettin' sort of crowded up here, maybe we can rent 'em out?" Immanuel said, and the two of them chuckled.

"Pa's awake and he's hungry," Leah said at the door to the cabin.

"You tell him we're about to break the fast," Uzziah said.

———

The infection continued for the next few days and Immanuel was getting worried. He'd done all he could for the man.

"We're gonna build a sweat lodge today."

"You know how?" Uzziah asked.

"Well, yeah, I told ya, I lived with the Paiutes for a while, got me a good edumacation with them, everything from wild herbs to this form of medicine."

They spent the day clearing a spot in the back of the cabins. They took saplings and bent them to make a dome-shaped structure. Then, they covered the dome with all the blankets they could find. There was an entrance like on a teepee, and it was only covered with a blanket. Outside of the sweat lodge, Uzziah dug a hole in which he built a fire. When the fire was roaring hot, he placed a bunch of large rocks in the fire.

In the meantime, Immanuel stripped down to nothing but his breechcloth and went off to pray. He carried the red clay pipe, which had been given to him at a sweat, and some sage and eagle feathers. He stayed up on the rocks above the camp for a good hour, then he came down.

"Expected maybe yer face would be glowin' like Moses when he came down from Mount Sinai," Uzziah quipped.

"Well, let's not let everything depend on that," Immanuel said in an uncharacteristic manner. Uzziah realized then that he'd better take this ceremony seriously.

"You will be the man at the entrance, and when I call for hot rocks, you are to shovel one into the pit dug in the middle of the sweat lodge," Immanuel instructed Uzziah.

Theodore had been brought out of the cabin and he didn't look well.

"Leah, strip your pa down to his trapdoors and, Uzziah, you get naked except for yer britches, okay.

Leah, if yer goin' in with your pa, you need to be in something very light," Immanuel advised her.

She went back into the cabin, and when she came out, she was wearing nothing but chemise and French knickers, which were silky underwear with slits on the side. They were both white.

They all entered the sweat lodge. Uzziah went last in because he was the fireman in charge of the rocks and had to be closest to the door.

One large hot rock was passed in, and Uzziah was told to shut the flap. Immanuel threw some water on the rock and steam gathered in the small dome. It became harder to breathe.

"Don't panic with the heat, just breathe normally," Immanuel said as he packed the pipe he was holding with some tobacco, or at least that's what Uzziah figured it was. He held the pipe up in the four directions and then lit it. He drew in a healthy breath of it, then passed it to Theodore, who also took in the smoke. He held it for a bit, then released it. Leah's father passed the pipe to her, and she, too, partook, then it was Uzziah's turn. He drew on the pipe like he was smoking tobacco, and there was the taste of tobacco there, but also something else. He wondered what Immanuel was up to.

"Another rock, please," Immanuel asked Uzziah, and he thought the pipe had gone around three times before this new hot rock was called for, but he couldn't rightly remember. He passed in the rock, and then another was asked for and then another.

The dome was filled with steam, and Uzziah felt light-headed, then he thought he fell asleep.

———

Uzziah was mounted up on Shadow and the horse was in an especially good mood, he was snorting and frolicking around. Leah was there, and she was mounted on her paint, and Uzziah looked for Theodore and Immanuel. They were far away, under a solitary cottonwood tree which was beside a running brook. The water in the brook was so blue that, at first, Uzziah thought the sky was running down beside the cottonwood.

"Hey, let's go over there," Leah said and spurred up her paint.

Uzziah rode up easily beside her. She was still dressed in nothing but her French knickers and the chemise. He wondered what she was doing riding like that. She did have on her boots, and she looked very attractive with boots and underwear on. She smiled back at him, and he realized he'd been smiling the whole time.

They rode toward an oasis with palm trees. He knew what they were, he'd seen them in a fairytale book one of his younger sisters had. There was a tent by a clear pool. He followed her lead as she dismounted and tied her paint up to one of the palms. There was a nice bit of grass there, and the horses began chomping on it.

She motioned for him to follow her into the caravan tent, and when he was inside, she closed the flap, which made the tent dark and warm—like the womb, he thought, and had no reason why he would think that.

Meantime, Leah had laid down on a pile of pillows in the middle of the tent.

"Come, sit," she said to him, and he sat cross-legged like an Injun beside her.

"Why are we here?" he asked her. It was getting hotter, and he wished the breeze, which was blowing the flap of the tent open at times, was inside the tent.

"Let's open the tent," he suggested, but she shook her head, *no.*

He resigned himself that the woman he loved, wait a minute, since when did he love Leah? He thought about that and realized that he had loved her before they even met. How was that possible?

"My pa killed my lover," she said in a low voice.

"But he said you did it," Uzziah protested but was secretly glad it hadn't been her.

"He thought Jean Baptiste would go easy on me because the beatings were so evident, but that trapper and unofficial lawman of Fort Saint Vrain was best friends with the man who loved me, and ifn it's a woman who kilt him, well, then it's a woman who's gonna hang. So, we ran."

"Why did he beat you?"

"It was the whiskey. When he was sober, he was fine, but get too much hooch in him and he went crazed," she said, moving over closer to him.

"What are ya doin'?"

"What ya want me to," she said, batting her eyelashes like giant fans. He could feel the coolness of being close to her, so he moved closer and put his arm around her.

"I can protect ya," he heard himself saying, then she was sitting in his lap and her arms were around his neck, and the sweet pinkness of her mouth was open, and she placed her mouth on his, and her tongue was inserted into his mouth, and he let go.

They lay there, making love, and it reminded him of the woman whose name he was never to speak again, she was so loving and giving. When it came to an end, that is, when they both had had as much of each other as they could stand, he came up off the pillows and, grabbing her, stood. Standing there in that tent, they shook with the passion that passes through us when we have been spent. They lay back down in each other's arms and fell asleep for what seemed years.

"We have to go now," she whispered.

"Why?" he asked, his eyes still closed.

"My pa's dead," was all she said, and when he opened his eyes, he was sitting next to the flap in the sweat lodge and Leah was crying. Theodore Blacksmith was hunched over and not moving.

"What happened?" Uzziah asked Immanuel.

"Healing comes in many forms. One of them is death," Immanuel explained as he dragged Theodore from the sweat lodge.

"Hold it right there!" he heard someone say. He'd heard that voice before.

The flap was turned back, and for a moment, Uzziah remembered the oasis and the palms, but out there was nothing but lodge pines and ponderosas. Leah had heard the voice also, and she was digging her way out of the sweat lodge away from the flap entrance. She wriggled out, and there was another voice.

"Hold it right there, mademoiselle." She had been captured. He knew that she hadn't killed her lover now and was coming out of the sweat lodge to defend her.

"You two," Jean Baptiste said, "over here by the cabins. Keep an eye on them, Pierre."

"She didn't kill her lover!" Uzziah blurted out, and Immanuel looked at him like he was crazy.

Jean Baptiste Charbonneau looked at Uzziah, and he smiled. It wasn't a sneer. It wasn't because he thought Uzziah was a madman, it was for another reason.

"We know," Jean Baptiste said.

"How? What?" Leah was asking.

"Michael stayed alive for the rest of the day. He told us it was your pa, who, it looks like, paid for his crime with his own life," said the trapper/lawman, looking down at the inert form of Theodore Blacksmith.

Leah ran and threw herself on her father's body. "Oh Pa, they knew, they knew all along!" she said, lying on top of the man and sobbing.

10

They had said their goodbyes to Jean Baptiste and Leah had turned down the invitation to go back to the Vrain Trading Post. There were just too many bad memories there. She didn't know exactly what she was going to do in the mountains, but she wasn't going back to where her father and her had lived, that much she had decided.

"I'm so sorry to have brought all this trouble on you two," Leah said, apologizing to the two mountain men.

"It was more trouble for you than anybody, it seems to me," Uzziah said, then added, "Ifn ya want to bury yer pa up here, I know a good spot."

"Really?!" she asked excitedly.

Uzziah looked at Immanuel, who nodded.

"Yeah, really. It's summer, and I got the time."

Uzziah got Shadow from the place he'd tied him on a highline behind the cabins. He was sweaty like he'd been ridden a long way.

"Where ya been, boy?" he asked the stallion, almost expecting an answer.

Leah was back there gathering up her paint.

"Hey, look at this," she said to Uzziah, who walked over.

"He's all flecked up like he's been running hard," she said, running her hands over the horse.

"Yeah, so's Shadow," Uzziah said, looking between the two horses.

Both horses snorted at the same time, and both jumped up as far as they could, tied on the highline.

"They know something we don't know," Leah said.

A breeze blew and the way it caressed both of them, they looked at each other.

"Did you almost have a memory?" Uzziah asked her.

"I had it, I'm sure," she said, walking closer to him. "We were somewhere together, weren't we?"

"An oasis?"

"Tall trees with fans as branches?"

They looked at each other and she moved closer to him and put her arms around his neck. He looked at her strangely.

"I think we already did this, but let's see," she said as they both moved at precisely the same time toward each other and just as their lips were about to touch, Immanuel had walked around the cabins.

"Jean Baptiste forgot one of his gloves—" was all he got out as Uzziah and Leah pulled back from their kiss. Immanuel was standing there with the glove in his hand.

They stayed standing close to each other and looked at Immanuel.

Uzziah helped her mount up and as she pulled her

paint around to the front where her pa's body had been tied across his horse.

————————

"What the hell was in that pipe?" Uzziah asked as he rode up beside Immanuel on Shadow.

"Just some herbs."

"Uh-huh," Uzziah said and put his hand down, and the two men didn't shake, they held hands.

"Ya comin' back?"

"Oh yeah."

"With her?"

"Seems like."

"Oh?"

"She's..."

"Right," Immanuel said, and the two men pumped their hands twice and let go.

————————

Uzziah remembered one of the spots he'd seen when they were searching for ponds to trap the first year they were up there. It was a meadow that was surrounded by snow-topped mountains, and there was a small stream that wound its way through the valley. In the spring, there were blue columbine, heartleaf arnica, which Immanuel had harvested a bunch of so he could use them for pain relief, arrow-leaf balsamroot, heartleaf bittercress, elk's lips, sego lily, Indian paintbrush, and many others. Some of them were still blooming, but it was past spring and into summer.

By the time they got there, it was late in the afternoon. They pitched a tent that Uzziah had brought along. It was going to be a sunset burial.

They walked around the meadow together. He carried the spade. It was a big meadow, but when Leah saw the spot where the ponderosas gave way to a little pool that ebbed and flowed under the pines, she spoke up.

"This is it, this is the spot where I want my pa buried."

"You go get the horses, and I'll start digging," he said as he dug into the rocky soil.

He looked up after a bit and he could see that she was almost to where they had made their camp. She was something that he wasn't sure what to do with. She was good-looking, he liked her looks. She seemed smart enough, but why, he wondered, did so many women get involved with men who beat them? Maybe it was just the type of men who lived out here, but that couldn't be the case because he never felt like hitting a woman, and he was sure that Immanuel had never hit a woman. He would have to ask him if that was so.

Coming toward where he was musing and digging, Leah held the three sets of reins.

"I'm sorry ya had to get involved in what was happening. Sorta makes me feel guilty, ya know?" she asked and looked back at her pa's body as it was gently flopped on the back of his horse. Every good horse should have to take this trip, with their masters on their backs, bringing them to their graves.

"How ya doin'?" he asked her when she walked up with the three horses.

"Wow," she said, looking down into the hole he was

digging and all the rocks stacked to one side. "You have done so much. It didn't feel like I was gone that long."

"I like to dig," he said, leaning on the shovel and the sweat rolling down his body.

He threw his back into it and the dirt was flying. She stood there and admired him. He wasn't her type, if a girl can say such a thing, and she certainly felt like she did have a type, but they were always pendejos before it was all over. Maybe her type was a bad type. She looked back at Uzziah. He was tall, big in the shoulders and arms, his muscles rippled nicely when the shovel hit the dirt, and his waist was surprisingly firm for such a big man. She didn't notice that he'd stopped digging and was staring at her as she stared at him.

"Oh!" she said as she realized he was taking her in with his eyes.

"Yeah, oh!" he said, grinning from one ear to the other. He got out of the good hole he'd dug and walked over to the body of Theodore Blacksmith.

"Sorry, sir," was all he said as he lifted the body and carried it to the grave. With an amazing amount of respect, he slowly lowered the body into the hole and folded the blanket around him so that no dirt got in his face.

She cried the entire time it took him to fill the grave and stacked the big rocks around so that the varmints wouldn't bother his eternal rest.

When the grave was finished, he walked over and got the Bible from his saddlebags. He wasn't sure what he was going to read, so he simply let the book open to where it would.

Then they cried out to the Lord in their trouble, and he delivered them from their distress. He led them by a straight way to a city where they could settle. Let them give thanks to the Lord for his unfailing love and his wonderful deeds for men, for he satisfied the thirsty and filled the hungry with good things. Psalms 107:6-9

"Would ya like to say some words, fer yer pa?"

She shook her head and continued to cry.

"I didn't know ya for a long time. In fact, we barely got to know each other. But ifn your gal, your daughter here is an example of how ya brought her up, then I'll tell ya, ya did a fine job, Mr. Blacksmith. I wish Immanuel had been able to fix ya so ya coulda lived, but we were given a certain amount of days when we was born, and when they's up, they's up. My guess is, God knew ya better than I did, and ifn ya didn't wander too far from the way, he'll be glad to see ya," Uzziah said, and she went into his arms weeping.

———

That night, they slept in separate bedrolls. She was inconsolable, and he remembered his ma when she had given birth to one of his brothers, who was perfectly formed but delivered dead. She sat with the little coffin in the dining room for the longest time, until his pa had gone in and picked up the little box and carried it out under one arm like he had gone to the market and brought a loaf of store-bought bread.

She had followed him, keening and crying until she saw that all the other of their kids were gathered around a hole in the family cemetery. His pa had dug the still-born boy's grave right next to where they had already had a double headstone with his name on the left as you faced it and hers on the right. The small hole was deep, but when she realized when she was laid to rest, she'd be right next to Daniel, she had named the boy before he was born, and some said that was the bad luck that led to his death, but Ma and Pa were not that superstitious.

He looked across at Leah during the night. The fire was between them, and the red streaks that lined her face were the dead giveaway that she was still mourning. He wanted her more than life itself, and they had almost kissed back at Immanuel's, and then there was the sweat lodge—something weird happened there. He would take his time with this one. He thought of the one whose name he could no longer say and thanked the Father that he had brought that blessing into his life. He was sure that Leah would be another blessing, but he worried that he might be jinxed. Maybe all the women he would love would be doomed to an early grave? He didn't want to think that way, and his ma and pa would have been disappointed that he carried such notions.

He must have fallen asleep early in the morning, but when he awakened, she had completely changed.

———

The fire was built back up, and bacon was sizzling in the pan, and the Dutch, which he loved to cook with, smelled like there was something in there that was going to be good.

"Well, you sleepy head, I wondered when ya was gonna wake up?" she said, the biggest smile on her face. How could this be the same woman who mourned all night long?

He sat up and rubbed his eyes, and she was there, sitting right next to him with a cup of coffee for him.

"Thanks," he said as he sipped the good, hot liquid.

"You are welcomed," she said, then they both started to say something, and both stopped.

"No," Uzziah said, "you go first."

"I been thinkin'," she said.

"Yeah?"

"Yeah, you two mountain men got three cabins back there, don't ya?"

"Yeah, last time I counted."

"There's just two of ya, and that leaves one cabin sort of lonesome for company."

"Yer right," he said and took a big gulp of coffee. "I feel kinda bad for that lonely cabin."

"I could keep it company, ya know?"

"You? Really!?!"

"Yeah, I wouldn't even charge ya."

"Free cabin sittin' services, well, I'll be?" Uzziah said, grinning the entire time.

"What d'ya think *E* will say?"

"*E*—I like that!"

"What will he say about, ya know, me keepin' the cabin from being lonely?"

He put down the cup and took her in his arms.

"He'll love it," Uzziah said as the sun came over the top of the mountain to east. Its light flooded them with warmth and her hair shone like a light you might see in heaven as she wrapped her arms around him and hugged him back.

A LOOK AT BOOK TWO
MURDERING SAVAGES: A WESTERN DOUBLE

Trouble hunts them. The mountains test them.

Uzziah O'Bannon and Immanuel Jones have carved out a life as rugged Mountain Men in the vast, untamed **Western Frontier**. But freedom in the high country comes at a price—and survival demands more than just a sharp eye and a quicker draw.

When a deal gone sour in Nueva Mexico lands Immanuel on the wrong side of a hangman's rope, Uzziah must match wits with soldiers, outlaws, and vengeful Apache warriors just to keep them both alive. Their bond will be tested by betrayal, buried secrets, and the ghosts of their own mistakes.

But fate isn't finished yet. A drunken misstep leaves them bushwhacked, wounded, and stripped of everything but their grit—and each other. On foot and bleeding, they doggedly track the ruthless gang that robbed them blind and left innocents in their path. With the law on their tail and justice in their sights, the two mountain men ride a thin line between vengeance and survival.

This two-book bundle includes the next thrilling novels in the Uzziah Mountain Man series.

AVAILABLE SEPTEMBER 2025

ABOUT THE AUTHORS

He was good looking and could sell ice to eskimos. But ... writing asked something else from him. He would have to corral his interest in being free. Writing would take him to a place where he was tamed, but also able to actually tell a story.

After the first two weeks at the Yale School of Drama, he called the head of the playwriting department, Milan Stitt and told him he was quitting. Milan invited him to lunch at a nearby Mexican restaurant in New Haven. He told the man who had had plays on Broadway that he wanted to be a free writer. Milan smiled, then explained the way to freedom was always through discipline.

Something in him clicked and it all began to make sense.

Three years later, when he received his MFA in playwriting, he received the much coveted Cole Porter Prize for Excellence in Writing.

Enter a woman, years later, when the first 'J' in J.J. Bonham, Jack Bonham, had written thirty screenplays in 7 years and had one optioned which looked like it actually might be done.

Unlike Milan Stitt, this woman had no plays on Broadway, but was a divorced mother of four grown children. She loved soaps, and was an ardent watcher of the same. In the years of her devotion to watching she developed an uncanny ability to discern plot and analyze character. Uncanny, really better than any of his teachers at Yale.

They, Jack & Judy, the other 'J' in J.J. Bonham, married in Buffalo Springs, Colorado. While teaching elementary school in Denver they read the same novella and looking up and into each other's eyes, realizing something. They could do that.

Thirteen years later they had written nearly 200 novels. Westerns mostly because that was who they were – a misplaced couple from the 19th Century who saw life in a western justice sort of way. They danced in Virgina City, Montana. Dances from a different time and place, but still their time and place.

Now, they live in the Bitterroot Valley on five acres and looking out the office window as he puts this together for them, he can see the thunderstorm marching across the Sapphire Mountains. Earlier, sitting on the porch, she had said something about the crack of lightning years before as they said vows of love in Buffalo Springs. He remembered.